SOMETHING NEW

Andrea Murray

SOMETHING NEW

Andrea Murray

ISBN paperback 978-1-77400-015-1

ISBN ebook 978-1-77400-016-8

www.dragonmoonpress.com

Other Books by Andrea Murray
Vivid (Book One of the Vivid Trilogy)
Vicious (Book Two of the Vivid Trilogy)
Vengeance (Book Three of the Vivid Trilogy)
Omni (Book One of the Omni Duology)
Contra (Book Two of the Omni Duology)

FOR CHRIS

You never questioned my Grandpa Harry ghost stories,
and you've lived them with me every step of the way.
Love you always!

PART I

LEVITICUS 19:31
REGARD NOT THEM THAT HAVE FAMILIAR
SPIRITS TO BE DEFILED BY THEM.

PROLOGUE

How had I ever let it come to this?

I pulled the necklace from my pocket and ran my thumb over the surface of the pendant, circling the center stone and pressing hard enough to feel the prongs nip. The burn told me I'd succeeded in slicing into skin.

Squeezing my finger against the cut, I watched my blood drip onto each leaf of the clover's design, the bright scarlet running over the stone's facets and pooling in the creases of the leaves. I smeared the essence of my very life till the silver surface was nearly covered.

It had all started with my blood and this necklace, and now I would end it.

CHAPTER 1

"Tell me again why I have to be here." Jake slumped against the doorframe's elaborate molding and pulled his phone from the pocket of his Crimson Tide hoodie. "I don't wanna miss the beginning of the game. Alabama's playing Arkansas today."

Football was life to my brother, and I almost felt sorry for him until I remembered he was the reason Mom had dragged us both along to this estate sale. He towered in the doorway, his 6' 3" frame somehow making the cavernous room seem smaller. The charging elephant and enormous "A" on his black sweatshirt was definitely out-of-place against the backdrop of Victorian-style wallpaper.

I ran my finger along the edge of the vintage mahogany wainscoting before yanking out his right earbud. "It's hours before the game starts, and besides if you hadn't gotten in trouble, we'd both be at home, ignoring each other right now instead of helping Mom scour this sale for bargains with a bunch of middle-aged antique junkies."

Last Friday night, Jake had decided riding around with his buddies after the game was more important than meeting curfew, and our parents had decided he needed a two-week grounding and more family time. The trouble was more family time for Jake meant more family time for me, too, a deterrent for the sins they assumed I wanted to commit. I crossed my arms. "I had stuff to do today, too."

"It was just thirty minutes. Not my fault they flip out over every little thing." He shrugged, slipping the earbud back in and reaching into his pocket again for the pack of cookies he'd stashed before we left home. "Also, not my fault with all that brain power you couldn't talk your way out of this—" he tilted his chin in Mom's direction where she was inspecting a large, blue and white patterned serving dish "—waste of a Saturday, and your studying isn't nearly as important as the game. We've been doin' this since 6:00! How much junk do we have to see in one day? I've got twenty bucks and a date with Leah on the line." He opened the cookie pack and shoved two mini-cookies into his mouth, ignoring the crumbs left on his shirt.

I curled my lip and raised a brow, swiping at the crumbs. "You bet on a date? You're disgusting. Does she even know you bet on who'd take her out?"

"Who do you think made the bet?" He wiggled his brows and popped in another cookie. "She likes a chase."

I rolled my eyes. "You deserve each other. What about Rachel?" Rachel had been my best friend since we moved here, and she had a huge crush on my sports-addled brother. He'd promised me he'd take her out after I helped him finish a paper on Charles Dickens. She'd already bought a new outfit and was probably hoping for a text that didn't seem likely to be coming. "And stop eating in here. You're being disrespectful and leaving a mess."

"Ria—" he shook his head and shoved his phone back into his hoodie pocket "—she's—"

"She's what?" I held up a finger. "She's cute." I held up another, counting off Rachel's good points the way I had when I'd finally gotten him to agree to take her out. "She's smart, and she's sweet. She isn't devious and trashy. She'll be a total change to what you're used to." I smirked and scrubbed a hand over his unruly brown curls. "And you promised."

"I didn't say *when* I'd take her out. She's a kid, and let's face it, she's nerdy. It'd be like dating my sister." He shivered, his face twisting, then held up the cookie pack wrapper to show it was empty.

I grabbed the wrapper and shoved it in my messenger bag. "She's seventeen, the same age as me—"

He threw up both hands. "Exactly!"

To Jake, the eleven months that separated us might as well have been four years. He constantly reminded me that I was the baby, and thus, less important than the firstborn. He called me the "backup" when he felt generous; more often he called me the "mistake."

"And there is nothing wrong with studying. You should try it sometime." He opened his mouth, but I held up a hand. "I know; the quarterback doesn't need good grades."

He grinned, that grin that managed to get him whatever he wanted most of the time. His light-brown curls covered his brows when he wiggled them. "It's called talent. Too bad you don't have any."

"And what happens if you can't play?"

He flipped his hand toward Mom. "Like she doesn't have a plan for that. Who do you think you get it from? She's probably already got my first semester planned out and written a check to pay for it just in case."

"Guess we really shouldn't complain." I watched Mom replace the bowl with a shake of her blonde head and hitch up the straps of her backpack as a well-dressed woman in black slacks and a purple blouse walked up and extended her hand. "The shop is the reason you drive that insanely large truck you used to get us in trouble."

My parents loved antiques, not in a "what a charming grandfather clock" kind of way but a "who needs a college fund" obsession. I seriously think sometimes they'd trade Jake and me for a Louis the XVI writing desk or a turn-of-the-century Tiffany lamp. In fact, you might say my brother and I exist because of their love for all things old. They met at an estate sale just like this one. Mom was fresh out of college, starting her own antiques shop, and my dad was a graduate assistant in the history department of a local university. He'd been hired by the family to help organize and catalogue the items, and she was looking to stock the shelves of her fledgling business, a business that became wildly successful and had forced our move two years ago. Mom had wanted a bigger shop in a larger community with space to expand, and she'd needed it. She'd recently hired yet another new sales associate just to accommodate weekenders.

Every time we got dragged along, they forced us to listen to the story of how they met. There's only so much hand-holding and blush-inducing whispering a kid should be forced to watch from her own parents, and the idea that a day spent contemplating dead people's crap made them so excited was just weird. But it's her life, and though Dad was now a professor, he was as crazy about 'hunting history' as she was.

"Go see how much longer." Jake poked his finger into my shoulder, nudging in Mom's direction. "They'll get mad if I ask again, and we'll be here forever."

I gave him a sharp look, but I had to agree. I'd just never tell Jake that. I adjusted the strap of my bag and tugged at my cream sweater. My boots thudded against the shiny hardwood. This was one of the more impressive stops we'd made today. Mom and Dad weren't above scouring flea markets and yard sales, but places like this were where they found the good stuff. Despite my agitation, I had to admit this was a beautiful house.

Dark wood gleamed in the October sunlight filtering through the stained glass window. Muted reds, blues, and yellows highlighted family heirlooms baring garish white and gold price tags. Some of the tags were stamped "Sold."

Estate sales had the choicest bits, but they always made me

sad, which was why I'd stopped coming with my parents years ago. Once I'd actually enjoyed a day out with them, getting ice cream at the end of our trekking all over the place, but when I was old enough to realize the majority of sales like this one involved someone dying, it all became macabre. I mean, we were digging through someone's treasures, a lifetime of accumulating things to love. And now that the owner was dead, his or her family was selling them off to the highest bidder.

I stopped beside my mother and the woman, who smiled briefly at me before turning back to Mom. My mother's blonde curls bounced as she nodded and crossed her arms. Like me, she was short, and this woman loomed over us both by four inches. Her makeup was perfection, and the two women couldn't appear more different with Mom's light freckles and soft blue eyes. On "scour days," she usually just slipped on comfy shoes, jeans, and a nice shirt with her ubiquitous backpack. But fancy clothes or not, Rebekah Gabriel was a force of nature, a hurricane in moccasins.

When I touched her arm, Mom shifted her eyes to me. "Oh, Miriam, I'd like you to meet Mr. Ezra's great-granddaughter, Angel Ezra. She's helping with his estate and is hosting the sale."

I nodded, reaching for the standard response I'd been taught long ago. "I'm sorry for your loss. You have some beautiful items." I gestured to the cherry mantel clock on the table before me. It had always been important to my mom, and eventually to me, to make a good impression. Impressions were everything. It didn't matter who you were on the inside, the outside was what people really cared about, and that outside had better seem intelligent, or the inside would never have a chance.

"Oh, thank you. We hate to part with it all, but—" Angel sighed, then smiled "—but Great-Granddad was a bit of a hoarder."

My mother smiled. "Is it hoarding when they're antiques?"

"It is when you have to ship it nine hundred miles. We've kept a few things, but the rest of the family isn't really into this kind of thing, and my grandparents are living in a retirement community in California, so here I am." She shrugged. "It's time for someone else to enjoy Jonathan's things."

I wondered how ol' Jonathan would feel about strangers crawling around his house, pawing his stuff. Thomasville, Alabama, wasn't a small town, but it wasn't so large that I didn't know about the reclusive Mr. Jonathan Ezra. My mom and I had driven by this place many times when she insisted we take the long way home from school. She'd even stopped in a few times to see if Mr. Ezra was interested in selling anything. I've never been inside the house with her, but every time she'd talked about it, her eyes sparkled, and I could easily picture her trying to reason with that wrinkled little man while she mentally inventoried each item she could spot.

"Well, I'm sure you won't have trouble selling any of it." I looked past Jake where he still stood in the doorway, giving me a hurry-up look, and could see a number of collectors I knew from the business.

"Let me know if you have any questions," Angel said as she walked past me and Mom. Jake smiled at her and watched her walk past him into the foyer, where she stopped to shake hands with a couple admiring an antique table near the door.

Turning back to Mom, I gave her my brightest smile. "So, I probably know better than to ask, but do you think we'll be going soon? I really wanted to stop by the bookstore and pick up another ACT prep book."

Raising a brow, she gave me the you-can't-be-serious look. "No way I'm missing this opportunity, and you already have two, so you can go tell Jake—" she leaned over to glance around me "—to stop sending you to ask. You can sit in the car if you like or better yet go find your father and tell him I need his advice and hurry!" Holding her finger close to her chest, she pointed surreptitiously toward an older woman in a blinged-out tracksuit. She was studying a landscape painting hanging on the wall opposite us. She lowered her voice to a harsh whisper. "That's Naomi Levi, and she'll buy everything worth having if we don't get on the ball."

I rolled my eyes but nodded. When I reached Jake, his brows raised in a hopeful look. I smacked him on the chest. "It's gonna be awhile, Bub," I said, using my childhood name for him that he pretended to hate. I passed him and walked toward a room with a table that looked large enough to seat the entire faculty in our high school.

"Excuse me," I mumbled, squeezing around a white-haired older woman who was admiring an enormous urn situated between the table and the door, but the woman stepped backward, and I knocked my hip against the corner of the table, grunting with the throb that shot down my leg.

"Oh, dear! I'm so sorry!" She swung around, her leather purse connecting with my stomach. She grabbed my upper arm to steady us both. "Honey, are you okay?" She laughed, and the bluest eyes I'd ever seen twinkled in the wrinkles of her face. "I am such a klutz!" Releasing me, she tugged her purse strap higher on her shoulder, her heavy silver bracelets clinking together as she moved her arm.

I smiled back and rubbed my hip. "I'm fine. No harm done."

She cocked her head, narrowing those mesmerizing eyes slightly. "Well, aren't you just about the prettiest thing. Such bright green eyes! How old are you, darling?" The deep red of her shirt mirrored the red of her lipstick.

My hand went self-consciously to the blond hair I'd hastily pulled into a clip this morning. Despite my mom's grooming, something about the question took me aback as a shiver ran down my spine. I could practically hear my mother's voice telling me not to be rude to a harmless old lady, but years of scary movies and urban legends raised a warning flag, and she must have seen it on my face because she quickly touched my forearm and shook her head.

"That must have sounded dreadful. I only ask because I have a granddaughter I suspect is close to your age, and I've found something I think she might like, but I'm just not sure. Would you mind taking a look at it?" Though the woman's smile never faltered, she slid her hand down my arm and touched my hand, tugging it slightly toward her. Her cold fingers gripped my hand harder than I would have given her credit.

I glanced at our joined hands and gave a small tug, but she tightened her grip, her glittering eyes focused intensely into mine. Her touch felt …wrong, and I just wanted to get away. "Well, uh, I'm supposed to be looking for my dad."

"Oh, it won't take long, dear. It's over here." She pulled me along with her toward a make-shift jewelry display case set up on the table.

"But my mom sent me to find—" I looked behind me as she dragged me along, hoping I could catch my brother's eye for a quick rescue. Harmless or not, the old lady's insistence was unnerving.

"Here it is." She pointed down to a gold ring on a dark green display stand. The square center stone was a deep blue and surrounded by small, round diamonds. "I think it's so lovely, but what do I know about you young people?" She patted my hand again, staring at me intently. "I don't even remember what it was like to be your age much less whether I'd have liked this then or not. So what do you think? Too much?" She wrinkled her brow even more than it already was, narrowing those blue eyes. In that moment, it felt as though she was somehow looking through me, and goosebumps ran down my arms. All I wanted to do was get away from this creepy woman.

I looked down at the ring again. It was a huge piece. I hardly ever wore jewelry, usually just earrings and a watch, and this was definitely not something I'd consider for myself, but one look at the woman's face showed how excited she was about the possibility of giving this ring to her granddaughter. "It's beautiful, ma'am, but I may not be the best person to ask. I hardly have any jewelry at all."

Her mouth dropped open, and she waved her hands around. "Sweetie, a pretty girl must have pretty things!" I noticed for the first time that she wore several rings and a large-faced gold watch. She patted my cheek, her skin cold and papery against my face, and I realized then that she hadn't stopped touching me since she'd bumped into me. I stepped back, but she took hold of my wrist, her fingers slipping beneath the fabric of my sweater and igniting the goosebumps again. Her eyes widened as she blinked slowly. "Looks fade, but jewelry lasts forever."

A young man in a suit approached us and pulled a key from his pocket. "May I show you something from the case?"

Her long, red nail tapped the glass of the case. "Yes, let me see that sapphire ring."

"Yes, ma'am, very nice piece, one karat with another half karat of diamonds set in fourteen karat gold. It's pricey but well worth the expense. We think it belonged to the owner's wife."

She grabbed my hand again and slid the ring onto my finger. It was a perfect fit.

She exclaimed, one hand going to her chest, the other still clutching my hand. "My granddaughter will love it." She scanned the case and pointed again. "And let me have that silver necklace as well."

The man pulled out a sterling silver rolo chain with a charm dangling from it. He held it up, and the woman took the chain in her hands, finally releasing me. Resting in her palm was a silver four-leaf clover about an inch and a half in diameter. In the center was a dark stone, but when she tilted her hand, the stone exploded with color, like a rainbow trapped in a cave. Blues, pinks, and oranges leapt to life in the middle of the solid silver leaflets. She held it close to my face.

"A black fire opal?" she asked, without looking at the man. Her eyes went to mine again.

"Yes, ma'am, nearly a karat. The silver gram weight—"

She waved her hand back at him. "Yes, yes, it's a heavy piece." She pointed to the indention in each leaflet. "Look at the detail. It even has a stem. And that stone! Gorgeous!" She held the chain against my sweater before unclasping it and fastening it around my neck. I touched the pendant where it hung just below the base of the neck. "I'll take that, too." She pulled her wallet from her purse and extracted a wad of hundred dollar bills, flipping through them until she'd counted out what I guessed was the amount for both and handing them to the man.

He smiled at the commission he no doubt would pocket. "Excellent. Let me get you a receipt." He turned and walked through the doorway.

I slipped the ring from my finger and handed it to her, but as I reached up to unclasp the chain, she waved her hand at me. "Keep it. Every girl needs jewelry. Jewelry will never let you down, especially a four-leaf clover. It's good luck."

I fumbled with the clasp. "But I couldn't—" My fingernail finally caught the latch, but it slipped.

She waved me off again and slid the ring onto her finger. "Yes, you can." She checked her watch. With a gasp, she said, "Oh my, I'm late! Bye, Miriam, thank you for your help." She turned for the door.

"No! Wait, I can't take this!" I tried to round the table and unlatch the necklace at the same time, but I caught my foot on a chair leg, and before I could catch myself, I was on my knees on the very expensive rug.

"What are you doing?" Jake stood smirking in the doorway. "Why are you on the floor?"

"Catch that old lady!" I pushed myself up and rushed toward Jake, who didn't do anything besides glance over his shoulder.

He pulled out his earbuds. "Who?"

"The one you just passed in the hallway." I pushed past him toward the foyer. I bumped into a couple who'd stopped to admire a large painting of a man wrestling a lion. When I finally reached the open door, I shielded my eyes against the sunlight streaming inside and scanned the street. Several people were getting into or out of cars parked along the long, tree-lined driveway, but there was no red-shirted old woman in sight.

"Who are you looking for?" Jake asked from beside me.

"A woman in a red shirt, white hair. You had to have passed her when you came into the dining room." I turned to him and lifted the pendant still around my neck. "She bought this, put it on me, and took off."

"Excuse me." Jake and I turned in unison to see the salesman standing behind us, a pink slip of paper in his hand. "I have the receipt for the ring and the necklace. Where's your grandmother?"

Jake's brow furrowed when he looked at me. "Grandmother?"

I shook my head. "She's not my grandmother, and she just took off." I shrugged. "I was looking for her, but she seems to have already left."

The corners of his mouth dipped. "She didn't get her receipt." He looked at the paper as though it might explode in his hand.

"What should I do with it?"

I lifted my shoulders again. "I'm not sure. She said she was late and had to go. Maybe she'll be back?"

He glanced again at the paper. "If you see her, tell her I'll keep this until the end of the sale." He smiled. "If you need anything else, please let me know, and thank you," he said over his shoulder, already moving toward the couple admiring the painting.

"An old lady bought you a necklace?" Jake picked up the charm and ran his finger over the surface. "Cool, I guess." He plugged in his earbuds. "Mom's looking for you." He stepped away toward the main room where I'd left Mom.

As I stared at his hoodie, I thought back to what the lady had said before she vanished. Something about what she'd said wasn't right. I fingered the pendant, remembering the intensity of her gaze and the way she'd touched me almost continuously. Then it hit me. She'd called me Miriam.

CHAPTER 2

"But, Mom, I don't want it," I said from our SUV's backseat. I touched the pendant where it still hung around my neck.

"Honey, it's lovely. I hate that we couldn't find that kind woman and thank her for it." Mom glanced in the rear-view mirror and met my eyes.

"But what about how she'd known my name? That's weird, right?"

"She's probably a customer of mine who's seen you in the shop." Mom flipped on her blinker and checked her mirror before changing lanes.

"But you said she didn't sound familiar." I'd found Mom immediately after searching the parking lot for the old woman and told her what had happened. She'd oohed and awed over the necklace, rambling on about the design and checking it for makers marks and how she thought it was over a hundred years old, blah, blah, blah—completing missing the fact that I was freaked out about the disappearing woman.

"Miriam, do you know how many elderly women I've sold pieces to in the last nineteen years?" She raised her brows.

"No, Mom, do you?" I crossed my arms.

She raised one brow. "Attitude, young lady."

"Sorry," I mumbled. "It was strange.. *She* was strange." I threw up my hands. "It creeped me out. I'd just like to give it back if we can find her. Maybe she came back after we left. We should go back and check."

"I looked for her, remember?" Dad said. He had gone on a brief search asking if anyone might know her, but after a half hour, he'd shrugged and suggested we pay for our items and hit a few more sales before lunch. "We still have two sales I want to check out." Dad held up the newspaper where he'd circled the day's prospects. Isaac Gabriel looked more like one of his students than a university professor with his brown curls and blue v-neck sweater, especially when his green eyes sparkled behind his glasses at the prospect of finding a hidden treasure.

"You said that two houses ago. Can we eat now?" Jake whined from the seat beside me.

"Jake, relax. That's my next stop, and, Miriam, I already told you I'd make some calls next week and see if some of the other shop owners might know her." Mom shook her head as she turned the SUV into the parking lot of Bethany's Burgers, Jake's favorite restaurant. I guessed she was trying to make up for keeping him out all day even though he was supposedly being punished. Mom can't stay mad. It's one of the things I loved and hated about her.

"Sweetie, it's beautiful. Just be happy and grateful," Dad said. His overlong, brown curls bounced as he shoved his crinkled paper beside the seat and unbuckled his seatbelt.

"Yeah, you're being dumb. Who doesn't like a gift even if it was a weird, old chick? Be glad someone likes you. " Jake smirked at me, then unbuckled his own seatbelt and opened his door.

"Not helpful, Jake." Mom turned to face me. "It's a little something new, honey, not anything to worry about." She opened her door. "Grab my wallet from my backpack please."

I watched her close her door and walk into Dad's arms for a hug before I reached down for her backpack where it lay on the floor at my feet. The clover pendant swung forward when I bent to unzip the bag, and the stone caught the sun, splashing mini-rainbows on the back of the seat in front of me. I ran my hand against the leather, the rainbows dancing across my skin, and remembered the way the old woman had gripped that same hand. Her cold touch, her brilliant eyes, the way she'd known my name even though I hadn't introduced myself—the meeting wouldn't leave my mind. I couldn't brush it off like Mom and Dad suggested.

A bang against the glass beside me made me jump. "What're you doing? Hurry up. I'm starving." Jake's face filled the glass.

I grabbed Mom's wallet and waved it at the window. "I'm coming, okay?"

Jake shook his head and mumbled something about being the slowest person alive as he turned back toward the restaurant's entrance where Mom and Dad waited. I touched the clover where it lay against my sweater. This definitely felt like more than something new.

****

"I'm going to watch the game." Jake kicked off his shoes and set down Mom's bags on the round cherry table in the center of the foyer. Lowering his hood, he shook out his curls like a wet dog. Right after lunch, the sky had clouded over, and a light rain had fallen on us as we made our last two stops.

"I've told you more times than I can count to stop leaving your shoes in the doorway." The wet rubber soles of Jake's shoes squeaked across the tile when Mom kicked them to the side as she put down the two bags she was carrying.

Dad struggled as he balanced a painting of a little girl in a field of daisies on top of an iridescent blue vase. He used his foot to close the heavy oak door. The painting teetered, and Mom ran over to catch it. "Careful, honey." She set the painting on the table. "I'll go get the rest."

Dad set down the vase beside the painting. "Just wait. I'll get it all later when the rain stops. I'm going to work on the connecting door to the garage, see if I can get it unstuck. Jake, come help me."

25

"But what about the game?" Jake complained. He tugged his damp sweatshirt over his head and dropped it on top of the painting, revealing his white t-shirt underneath.

"Record it. Come on." Dad put his arm around Jake, who rolled his eyes.

"Watching a recording isn't the same, Dad."

"No, and neither is a full weekend in your room." Dad smiled as Jake dropped his head.

"That door's been messed up for a week. It'll be okay for a few more hours. I promise to help without complaining when the game's over. That's reasonable, right?" He cut his eyes at Dad and grinned.

"No dice, pal. Let's go." Dad gave him a little push down the hall. "It'll be great father-son bonding time."

"More like cruel and unusual punishment," Jake grumbled. But Dad laughed and patted Jake's shoulder as they started toward the garage door.

I put Mom's backpack on the table. "You need help?"

"I got it. You go on." She pulled the painting from beneath Jake's hoodie and began tilting her head as she examined it closer. I knew she'd be lost in her purchases for the next couple of hours, searching the net to find out more about each one so she could talk some future customer into buying it.

"I'm going to my room for a while." My feet were hurting, and I wanted to change clothes and snuggle under my blanket for an hour in the solitude of my room. I started to lift the strap of my bag over my head on my way to the mahogany staircase that had been such a selling point when Mom and Dad were house shopping.

"Oh, Miriam, before you go upstairs, will you feed Cain?"

"Now?" It was my turn to complain. Cain was our German Shepherd—no, not really *ours*, more like *theirs*. About three years ago, one of Mom's faithful customers who was a dog breeder had offered the pick of the litter in exchange for a bureau. Mom had never had a dog when she was a kid, and even though Jake and I were a little old for the whole first pet thing, she'd made the trade. I guess as dogs go he was okay. The breeder had supplied an impressive pedigree and gone on and on about his champion sire, but Cain and I never really clicked. He wasn't aggressive towards me, but he wasn't gaga about me like he was with Jake, who typically took care of him.

"Yes, now." Mom glanced at me. "He's a member of this family, too, and Jake's busy with your father."

I suppressed the urge to talk back and settled for an eye roll before trudging through the arched entryway that led to the kitchen. Mom loved to cook, and since she spent so much time in the kitchen, she'd painted it marigold because she said it made her happy, and though "vintage" was her life, the kitchen was modern. The stainless steel appliances looked strange next to her hundred-year-old buffet and matching table, but the whole place was perfectly suited to my mother.

Across the kitchen were the French patio doors. I stopped at the huge stainless steel trash can where Mom stored Cain's food, stepped on the foot pedal that opens the lid, and used the scoop inside to dip out some food before I unlocked the doors. Peeking outside, I couldn't see him anywhere, so I assumed he was inside his house. Cain spent his days outside in the fenced backyard where Dad built him a doghouse big enough for two dogs.

Light rain pattered on the concrete patio. I wasn't exactly happy about going out in it again. "Cain!" When I called, he poked his long black muzzle expectantly from the doorway of his house. His ears perked for a second before he fully realized it was me and not his beloved Jake. "Come on. I've got your food." I shook the plastic measuring cup, rattling the food inside to coax him out. Mom likes for him to eat at least an hour before we bring him inside for the night to make sure he has time to do his business. But he pulled his head back in, uninterested in my offering.

I stepped closer to his bowl, crinkling my nose at the water that had collected inside before I dumped it, then put his food inside. When he heard the food fall into the bowl, he stuck his head out again. "Come on, you know Mom will be mad." As if he understood, he slipped from his house, stretching his long legs in front of him before full-body shaking and sending up a cloud of hair. That's one reason he stayed outside part of the time—a coat that never seems to stop shedding. Mom says she can only stand a part-time inside dog. I reached out to rub his ear, but he backed up a step. His ears stood alert as he cocked his head.

"Oh, now you don't want me to pet you?" I stepped toward him again, and he backed up, like some weird dance. "What's wrong with you?"

Cain barked loudly, the way he does when someone rings the doorbell. Cain's bark fit his size. At almost ninety pounds and with paws the size of my hand, he wasn't exactly small, and that bark usually managed to make visitors back off the porch. Even though I'd heard it a million times, it always made me jump. The measuring cup fell from my hands and clattered on the patio.

"Cain!" I snapped my fingers like Mom does when she wants him to hush. Not missing a beat, he continued to bark. "Cain, stop!"

"What'd you do to him?" Jake asked from the patio door.

"Me? I didn't do anything. He's freaking out."

Jake walked toward Cain. "What's the matter, buddy?" He held out his hand, and Cain jogged to him, licking his hand before dunking under it for the ear rub I was going to give before he completely flipped his lid. Jake knelt while Cain licked his face. "Yeah, he just missed me, didn't you?"

"Aren't you supposed to be fixing something?" I crossed my arms.

"Dad said I could go watch the game." He peeked over his shoulder at me. "The trick is to get in the way more than you help. Works every time." He turned back to Cain and nuzzled against his head before standing. "Wanna watch the game with me?"

I bent to pick up the cup I'd dropped when Cain started barking. "I've got work to do."

His brows dipped when he looked at me before he grinned. "I was talking to the dog. Come on, Cain." He moved toward the door, but Cain stood his ground, facing me again and barking wildly when Jake stopped next to me.

Jake and I exchanged looks. "Man, you really pissed him off. What'd you do?" he repeated.

I threw up my free hand. "I didn't do anything. He's never liked me. I don't know why Mom sends me out here."

Jake whistled, then patted his thigh. "Let's go, buddy. Inside." But Cain took a step closer; his bark echoed. "It's okay, Cain. Nobody likes her." Jake shot me a grin.

"Funny. I'll go in, and maybe he'll calm down." I'd have to go around Jake to get inside, but I really didn't think going between him and his hairy best friend who seemed to hate me at the moment was such a great plan, so I tried to squeeze between Jake and wall of the house. When I did, I put my hand on Jake's back to nudge him forward.

Cain went crazy. He charged toward us. I squealed and cowered behind Jake, peeking over his shoulder to see snapping jaws and flying slobber.

"Jake! Do something!"

Jake grabbed Cain's collar and jerked him away. "Cain, no! What's wrong with you!"

I didn't waste any time. I skidded inside the kitchen and slammed the door.

CHAPTER 3

"What is going on?" Mom's voice made me spin around and my heart pound even harder.

I grabbed her arm and dragged her to the door to watch Jake trying to calm Cain, who was still barking and lunging toward me. "The dumb dog lost it! He tried to attack me!"

"What? That doesn't sound like him. What did you do to him?" She glanced between me and the dog, now panting on the other side of the glass as Jake rubbed his ears.

"Why does everyone assume I did something? Jake said the same thing. He just went nuts! He barked and barked, then when I touched Jake he flipped! If Jake hadn't been standing there, he'd have killed me."

Mom's lips flattened as her brows dipped. "You're exaggerating, Miriam. Cain would never attack you."

"Mom, he hates me, always has! Now it's just official." I threw up my hands and slipped my messenger bag over my head, and it snagged on the necklace that I'd forgotten I was wearing. I touched the silver pendant. "This has been the weirdest day. First, a creepy old lady buys me a necklace I don't want, and then the dog tries to attack me."

"He didn't try to attack you, honey. I'm sure he was playing." Mom faced me and pointed to Cain, who had his big paw on Jake's forearm the way he always does when he wants to be petted. "See, he's fine now."

"Yeah, well, I'm not taking any chances. Jake's bringing him in, and I'm going to my room to take a shower." I turned to leave the kitchen.

"I'll call you when supper's ready."

I looked back at Mom's smiling face then through the door at Cain, remembering how he had looked with spittle flying and teeth bared. I could stand to skip a meal.

****

I used my towel to squeeze out the water that was still dripping from my hair and scanned my room for my favorite cupcake-covered pajama bottoms. Usually, I left my pajamas on the end of my bed after straightening the sheets and blankets, but I'd dressed in a rush this morning, scattering the nightclothes I'd wear again tonight to save Mom laundry.

This room was my sanctuary with its amethyst walls and purple and black brocade curtains. Dad had worried I'd turned Goth or emo when I decorated my room in such dark colors a year ago. For a month after I'd painted, I'd caught his sideways looks at the dinner table, checking for traces of self-imposed morose I suppose. But the colors suited me, made me feel calm. The almost obsessive straightening, well, that had escaped his notice. Keeping my life organized was a necessity if I wanted to be successful.

The demands I put on myself to study hard, make the top grades, and earn the respect of my teachers didn't make sense to Jake, but it was as much a part of me as football was of him. Mom and Dad weren't the cause of my drive, but they certainly didn't hate it. The belief that I'd earn a scholarship was pretty much a done deal, and I wouldn't disappoint either them or myself.

I grabbed the sports bra that I'd never actually used for sports from the chair where I'd left it and yanked it over my head and around my chest. I pulled clean underwear from the drawer, and as I shimmied into them, I finally spotted my pajama bottoms lying just under my bed and fished around next to them for my pink T-shirt. When I stood, I caught my reflection in the full-length mirror across from my bed. I touched the clover pendant where it hung at the bottom of my throat, the opal's fire dim in the muted light coming from my bedside lamp.

The sparkling blue eyes of the old woman crept into my mind. She'd been so insistent that I help her, and her hand had barely left me. Remembering the feel of her skin left me with an unexplained chill, and I rubbed my arms to get rid of the goosebumps. I unclasped the necklace, holding the pendant in my palm and feeling its warmth from where it had rested against my skin as the chain dangled from my fingers. When I moved my hand, bursts of orange and green shimmered in the stone where it nestled in the center of the silver leaves.

It was pretty, whimsical even, but I couldn't shake the feeling I'd gotten when she'd vanished. She couldn't have had a minute's head start when I tried to chase her down. Re-clasping the necklace again, I hung it from the left post on the mirror's stand and pulled on my shirt and pants as my cell phone chimed from the bedside table.

I crossed to the phone and slid my finger over the screen. A tiny circle with Rachel's photo appeared beside a message.

Rachel: *When are coming home?*

Me: *Already here. Want to come over?*

Rachel: *Yep! Movie and pjs?*

Me: *Of course. You pick the movie.*

Rachel: 😁

Rachel and I had been best friends since I came to Thomasville High sophomore year, and we had clicked from the day she'd volunteered to be my project partner in Pre-AP World English. We had to analyze a common theme in three of Edgar Allan Poe's stories and present our results. I'd only been at Thomasville for a few days and had to play catch up on the unit readings. Rachel took pity on me. As it turned out, we made a great team, busting through our analysis at my house every night for a week. It was during one of those 11:30 cram sessions that Rachel had admitted how much she liked Jake, explaining in great detail why she thought he should go shirtless every day. Eww.

So, despite my disgust, I'd been working since then to get him to take her out, and after the mess he'd made of his English paper, I thought I had him. I'd only agreed to help him after he promised to ask Rachel out but so far, nada. With each visit, she hoped he'd pay attention to her. Tonight, she'd come over in her cutest pajamas, her black curls threatening to overtake her smiling face, and walked in front of him as many times as possible until he left the room. Then she'd spend twenty minutes quizzing me on whether or not she had a shot.

Grabbing the ponytail holder off the table, I twisted my hair into a messy bun before plugging my phone into the charger and heading downstairs. I glanced at the family photos covering the antique red and gold wallpaper in the hall. Mom had spent weeks searching the Internet for the perfect paper and wall sconces. She'd chosen the paper and paint in each room to match what might have been there when the house was constructed in 1875. When I pointed out to the irony that she'd immediately covered so much of the surface with photos, she just laughed and said that it showed what's important to her, her family and her antiques.

Thinking about my earlier scare, I shook my head as I walked past the photo of Jake and Cain when he'd had been small enough to fit into the gangly teenager's arms. Jake's muddy T-shirt matched Cain's muddy paws, and he was smiling as Cain licked his cheek. That was the day we'd picked him up at the breeder's house, and they'd been fast friends ever since.

I stopped at the top of the stairs to listen for Cain, gripping the Art Nouveau lamp that stood sentinel on the newel post. The figure's bare breasts had been the catalyst of myriad jokes between Jake and his buddies, and despite Mom's history lessons on the awakening of women and Prohibition, the boys continued to routinely make comparisons with the girls they'd dated or wished they had.

I heard Jake screaming a protest at the television followed by a loud bark from Cain. Hearing that bark made my heart beat a little faster.

"Mom," I called, looking down toward the foyer table where she'd been sorting her purchases earlier, but I saw only the painting of the little girl. "Mom!"

The clunk of footfalls echoed on the hardwood floor in the direction of the kitchen. Mom emerged from the entryway, rubbing her hands on a dishtowel. Her blond ponytail swung as she looked around the foyer.

"Up here," I said, and she turned her face up, the furrow between her brows silently questioning why I was standing at the top of the stairs. "Is Cain going to try to kill me again if I come down?"

Mom shook her head and closed her eyes. When she looked up at me again, she had that "what is wrong with my children" expression that she usually wore when Jake said he didn't really need good grades because he'd be playing in the NFL someday. "Cain wasn't trying to kill you. You startled him or something. He's fine. He's in the family room with Jake."

"Rachel's coming over," I said to her retreating back as she turned and walked back toward the kitchen.

"Good," she answered, raising her hand and waving her fingers.

The stairs creaked as I walked down slowly. I wasn't taking any chances as I crossed the tile in the foyer and turned toward the family room. "Jake, is the dog in there?" I knew he was. I only asked to let him know I was coming in.

I tiptoed in the entryway, trying to peek over the back of the brown suede couch where Jake was lying with his head on the arm rest. The cheering crowd on the television was so loud I wasn't sure if he couldn't hear me or was just ignoring me. "Jake!"

"What, Ria?" He turned and looked at me around the couch back. "Hello! I'm trying to watch the game!"

"Is Cain in here?" At the mention of his name, I heard Cain's collar tags jingle.

He flopped his hand out toward the coffee table. "Yeah, he's right here."

I walked gingerly toward the couch as Jake turned his attention back to the game. When I was even with the arm where Jake's head rested, I could see Cain, lying between the couch and the coffee table. He raised his head, ears up, and looked at me, tilting his head left and right before lying back down. No snarling, no barking.

Jake reached down and rubbed his ears. "See. He's fine. He's forgotten whatever it was you did to him." Jake picked up his glass of sweet tea with one hand and crammed his other into a ravished bag of chips beside him.

"I didn't—oh, never mind. Rachel's coming over. Are you about finished?" I gestured toward the television and the food mess I'd have to clean up before being able to relax.

"It's the fourth quarter." He pointed toward the score bar at the bottom of the screen showing Alabama ahead by seven, as the clock ticked down from three minutes. "I missed part ofthe first half but looks like we're gonna win."

I pumped my fist in mock celebration. "Awesome. So, did you win your bet with Leah?" I asked, remembering our earlier conversation at the Ezra sale.

"Of course, but she knew I would." He wiggled his eyebrows.

I shook my head. "When do you pick her up?"

"Trying to get rid of me? I'm grounded, remember?" He sat up, and Cain stood. I backed up a step.

"Stop being a chicken. Come pet him. He's calmed down." Jake patted the couch next to him, and I sat, tentatively reaching out to Cain, who sniffed my hand then licked me. I rubbed his chest, and he put his big paw on my forearm.

"I just wanted to see if we could use the TV. You're welcome to stay. I'm sure that'd make Rachel happy."

Jake sipped his tea and shrugged. "Might be fun."

I raised a brow.

He smiled. "Girls night with my little sister and her friend who worships me. Could be worse."

I rolled my eyes. "You're incorrigible."

"And if I knew what that meant, I'd be as nerdy as you. Maybe Rachel will spend the night waiting on me." He jiggled his empty glass.

"Too bad she's not here now. Clean up your chips." I stood and walked toward the doorway. Rachel might get her shot, and as grossed out as that made me, I couldn't help but smile. This night might be okay after all.

CHAPTER 4

"Then she just vanished. I ran after her, but when I got to the door, she was gone. It was so weird." I turned back to Rachel Timothy where she sat cross-legged on my bed, examining the necklace. "I know it sounds stupid, but it kind of creeped me out."

I fiddled with the lid of my mostly empty jewelry box where it stood on my dresser. The gilded metal on the corners and around the top hugged the lavender fabric with just the right pressure. Turning the metal latch, I lifted the lid, and a tiny, dancing couple carved from ivory and wearing eighteenth-century costumes stood on a platform in the center, waiting in expectation for me to turn the key at the back and begin their dance recital. Touching the woman's minuscule white curls piled atop her rouged face and red lips, I thought of the red nails and crystal eyes of the old woman. An uneasy feeling crept into my stomach.

Rachel held the necklace up to the lamp beside the bed. Her black hair was pulled into a ponytail showing off her perfect profile, and she scrunched up her nose as she leaned closer.

Rachel was the sort of girl who is naturally pretty. Her full lips and big eyes made her a knock-out. The problem—according to most boys, Jake included—was her brain. Apparently, she intimidated them, which was almost too sexist to even consider possible. "It's pretty. What kind of stone is it?"

"Fire opal, that's what the lady said."

Rachel's honey eyes stared intently at the necklace as she let it twist in the light. True to form, she'd shown up in her pink gingham flannel pants and a pink sweatshirt with glittering white letters saying, "Cinderella is proof the right shoes can

37

change your life." Only Rachel would be so matchy-matchy in her jammies.

"Well, I think it's nice." She held it up to her chest.

I chuckled. "You think anything that sparkles is nice."

"And *you* think anything that sparkles makes your IQ go down." She stood and bounced off the bed. At barely five feet, Rachel was even shorter than me. Her baggy sweatshirt reached mid-thigh, and her pants nearly covered her white and pink toe socks. "A little shine never hurt anyone," she said, holding the necklace beside my face. "It brings out the green in your eyes."

Her words made me think again of the old woman. She'd commented on my eyes, too. I looked at my reflection in the small, framed mirror inside the jewelry box. The stone did look green; whereas, earlier, the opal had been a ray a colors, but Rachel was right. This close to my eyes it seemed to reflect their color. I closed my hand around the pendant, and Rachel let it drop. "I don't think that." I gently flipped her diamond huggie hoop earring. "I always compliment your jewelry, and you're the smartest person I know."

"It's a four-leaf clover. It's good luck. Wear it." She nodded, causing her ponytail to bob.

Just like the old lady had said. I rubbed the hair that had risen on the back of my neck, and dropped the necklace inside the jewelry box. Rachel stepped in front of the box and swiped her finger over the meager three pairs of earrings inside before picking up the only other occupant of the box, a twine and bead bracelet. She twisted the blue plastic beads on the orange string. Her full lips stretched to a grin. "What's this? Did a little boyfriend make it for you?"

I smiled. "Jake made it."

Her squeal made me wince. "Oh, he's the sweetest boy ever!"

"He was seven, Rach, and a complete jerk most of the time.

He made it for Mom, but it was too small, so he gave it to me. I overheard Mom telling him to." I watched as she twisted her hand and wiggled into the bracelet.

With a triumphant smile, she extended her wrist. "It fits!"

I shook my head as she reached into the jewelry box again and touched the tiny man in his painted, powder-blue breeches and matching waistcoat. "This box is so pretty, Ria. Why haven't you shown it to me before?"

I shrugged one shoulder. "It doesn't work anymore, but it did when Mom bought it for me. I was ten, and we were at an estate sale. It was a real wreck when she got it, but she had it restored." I scooted the box so that Rachel could see the back and touched the bronze key. "You turn this key, and it should play music while they spin around, but…" I shrugged again and turned the box back around.

"It's still pretty." Rachel tugged the bracelet and wiggled her hand until it sprang free. She squeezed it to her chest before dropping it back into the box.

I closed the lid and turned the latch. "Let's go see what Mom cooked."

Rachel grinned. "Can I sit by Jake?"

I started for the door, tossing over my shoulder, "Please do."

****

I tried to suppress my third yawn in ten minutes as I listened to Rachel giggling hysterical when Jake burped his name. I shot her a look that said I couldn't believe she actually laughed at that, but she shrugged and smiled at me, despite my mouthing, "Don't encourage him!" I knew she liked him, wanted to get his attention, but really?

One of those inspirational football movies was playing on the TV—Jake's choice of course—as though a team of inner-city kids who had just started playing football would ever really have a shot at a national championship. I snuggled deeper into the couch and tucked my feet behind Rachel. She was too consumed by Jake's gaseous emissions to notice.

I shook my head and looked at my cell phone screen. 11:30. I didn't try covering the next yawn. "I need to go to bed." I turned to Rachel. "You staying?"

"No, church with Gram tomorrow. Guess I need to head out." Rachel's sigh was as loud as Jake's burp. She wanted to stay, spend as much time flattering Jake as possible in hopes he'd ask her out. She stood and grabbed her phone as she cast a longing look at Jake, who smiled.

When Jake lowered the footrest on the recliner and stood, my brows rose involuntarily.

"I'll walk you to the door," he said.

Rachel's smile was so wide I was afraid her face might split. When she nodded, her ponytail bounced like a rubber ball on a string.

"Come on." Jake put his left hand in the middle of Rachel's back and gestured with his head toward the family room's doorway, and with that, I was completely forgotten.

"Bye, Rach." She didn't turn around, staring instead at Jake's profile beside her as they walked out. I'm pretty sure I heard her murmur goodbye. I slumped back to the couch and scrolled through my Instagram feed until I heard the door shut. I absolutely didn't want to see my brother's "game" with my best friend. I was the one who suggested they date because Rachel had wanted it so badly, but I supposed somewhere inside I'd thought it would never happen. To actually see Jake touching Rachel brought home how horrifically bad this could turn out. If he was true to form, he'd do the date and drop, and Rachel would be crushed.

When Jake walked back in, his enigmatic hint of a smile had

me questioning whether a relationship between Rachel and Jake was such a good idea. I didn't want to see Rachel hurt, and Jake was consumed by his unrealistic dreams of sports greatness and the female entourage that came with it.

I slid a narrowed look at Jake. "She's not a toy or a distraction. If you play with her feelings, I'll—"

"Relax, little sister." Jake lifted one hand and plopped down across from me in the recliner. "It was only a cheek kiss. I didn't break her heart."

"But you will, won't you?" I pointed my finger at him and leaned toward the recliner.

"Is it possible that I might actually like her? I'm not a complete jerk, Ria." When I crossed my arms and continued to stare, he sighed. "She's cute, okay?"

"She's more than cute. She's my best—probably my only—friend. Please don't hurt her."

This time Jake leaned toward me and ducked his head so that he glanced up at me. "I asked her on a date, like you asked. And I do like her. It's a meal. I won't intentionally hurt her." His half-smile wasn't as comforting as he was trying to make it.

I walked out, leaving Jake and my phone behind. Rachel would doubtless text half the night with happy emoticons of kissy faces and hearts. All the way upstairs, I regretted fostering Rachel's infatuation. I had a 4.0 GPA with four AP classes, but I couldn't see what a terrible idea it was for Jake to take Rachel to the movies and buy her a burger afterward? I was as mad at myself for being stupid as I was at Jake for the inevitable hurt he'd cause Rachel.

I scowled at Jake's photo, wishing I could knock it right off the wall and stomp on it. I was so preoccupied with my photocide that at first I didn't notice the music. Through the closed door of my bedroom came a tinkling, tinny sound.

I stopped, my hand on the knob. Why was the door closed? I only closed the door if I was inside. Years ago, I'd learned leaving the door open so Mom could see inside occasionally kept me off the no trust radar, not that I had anything to hide, and I mean sadly anything. And it also constantly left Jake on the hot seat, which was great, if not mean. Rachel must have closed the door earlier when we went down to eat. I'd left the lamp on, and the light shone from under the door.

I tried to turn the knob, but it didn't budge. I tried again, wiggling it, but nothing. Putting my shoulder against the door, I pushed and turned, but the door wouldn't budge. I put my ear against it, listening to the sound coming from within. It was a familiar tune but one I hadn't heard in many years. It sounded an awful lot like—creaking on the stairs had me turning toward the end of the hallway. Jake was on his way up. I wiggled the knob again as he walked closer.

"What's wrong, lock yourself out?" As he walked up behind me, the music stopped. He reached for the knob, and it turned easily in his hand.

I cocked my head and watched the door swing freely open. "Guess it was stuck. Maybe the rain made it swell?"

Jake shrugged. "Like the garage door. Don't tell Dad."

Jake was afraid Dad would put him to work again. "Don't worry. I have no intention of allowing you to work on my door." I walked in and scanned the room for the cause of the music. My phone was downstairs. My tablet was dead, and my laptop was closed. As I slipped off my pajama bottoms, I was about to dismiss it as my imagination when I glanced at the dresser. My jewelry box was open, the happy couple standing still in the center of the box. I thought back to earlier when Rachel and I had dropped the necklace inside. I was certain I closed the lid.

As I touched the lid, the lamplight shined in the tiny mirror, casting a mini spotlight on the couple and reflecting on the opal in the clover pendant. I turned the box around and twisted the key. The same tune I'd heard from outside my door, somehow sad and happy at the same time, pinged from the hidden mechanism. I hadn't heard the box play for more years than it had actually worked. I think it stopped working a year after Mom gave it to me, but I remember that tune, haunting. It used to make me cry, and Mom had almost hidden the key because it upset me so much even though I couldn't explain why I cried or stop listening to it either. When the music stopped, she'd refused to have it fixed.

Yet, here it was as if it had never stopped working.

Maybe Rachel was right. Maybe the clover was good luck after all. I smiled. I sounded completely crazy. I didn't believe in luck. Preparation and determination, that's what brought good fortune, not some piece of jewelry. It was more likely the rain that had caused the door to stick had revived the mechanism than that a hunk of cold silver had magically done it.

Coincidence—nothing more.

I watched the couple twirl in a circle for a second, then closed the lid.

CHAPTER 5

Sunday morning church was mandatory in the Gabriel household. I didn't really mind, though. Believing in something greater than myself gave me peace. It sounded crazy to a lot of people, but knowing the Big Guy was looking out for me helped with the pressure of school—another crazy idea to a lot of people.

When I was a kid, we went to Sunday school. My parents wanted me well-versed in Old Testament stories and New Testament parables, but as Jake and I got older, they decided preaching would suffice. Going to church kept me strong, and though I would have liked to think most of the other churchgoers agreed judging by the full pews, I suspected a lot of them went because it was expected, not because they were faithful followers. As I looked around the sanctuary from our back-row pew, I decided maybe socializing between Sunday school and preaching was the real reason.

Moms and daughters clearly dressed for post-service selfies leaned close to their neighbors, whispering less about scripture and more about who was caught stealing from the local Wal-Mart and whose boyfriend drove home drunk last night. Fathers in autumn-colored sweater vests picked out by their better halves shook hands then quickly shoved them in their pockets before complaining over the town's slow process in picking up the leaves their sons raked into piles near the curb before moving on to who should be running for mayor. Their sons peeked at their phones then at the girls across the aisle who had messaged them.

I fiddled with the clover charm necklace Mom had guilted me into wearing this morning. After she'd commented about fifty times how nice it was and how it would look cute with my blue tunic dress, I finally gave in and slipped it from my jewelry box. I'd glanced at the tiny figures and thought about turning the key to see if last night's strange experience had been all in my mind, but Jake's yelling for me to hurry stopped me.

Paul Shiloh, the principal at my high school, approached from a few rows ahead of us where he'd been shaking hands. His balding head caught the glint of morning sun from the windows. He smoothed the remaining red hair that rimmed his ears and the back of his head, straightened his navy tie, and reached for my father's hand. "Good morning, Gabriel family, isn't it a beautiful day?" He shook hands with Mom and Jake, and when he reached me, his megawatt smile grew. "And how's my star student today?"

I returned his smile. "Fine, sir." Mr. Shiloh had always been one of my staunchest supporters, asking me how my classes were and if I needed a letter of recommendation for anything.

"Been studying for the ACT?" Before I could nod, he shook his head and chuckled. "What am I talking about? Of course you have. You know Ms. Jordan is offering some after-school science tutoring for the exam if you're interested." He motioned toward an attractive brunette near the front. Ms. Eve Jordan was my AP physics teacher, and last year, she'd allowed me into her AP chemistry class even though the class was typically reserved for juniors and seniors.

"She hasn't announced it in class yet. When does it start?" I pulled out my phone to check my calendar and create a reminder.

He tilted his head, and his brow wrinkled. "Tomorrow, I think. You should run and ask her before singing begins." He nodded to my family and moved to the next pew to make the rounds.

"Mom?" I cut my eyes to her, and she nodded. Sliding from the pew, I straightened my blue tunic, pulling it securely over my tights before walking toward Ms. Jordan, who turned with a smile, her pink lips exactly matching her fuzzy pink, v-neck sweater. Though she was in her mid-forties, she was still pretty enough for the boys to flock to her room with more interest in the divorcée than science.

"Ria! How are you?" She patted my hand, and smiled with true concern. Ms. Jordan had become my favorite teacher last year with every genuine compliment and encouraging head nod. "Did you have a good weekend?"

"Yes, ma'am. Mr. Shiloh said something about ACT prep for science. Are you offering after-school tutoring next week?"

She nodded, her brown curls bouncing around her face. "We only just got approval Friday afternoon. I was going to announce it tomorrow morning. I take it you want to sign up?"

"Yes, ma'am," I repeated, smiling.

"Great! It may be just the two of us with such short notice, but I thought I'd try to schedule our first meeting for tomorrow afternoon."

"That would be fine with me." I stood. "See you tomorrow." Walking back toward our pew, I smiled at the thought of my scores going up another one or two points.

Mom scooted as I sat and opened my bag to make sure my phone was on silent. Rachel peeked at me and waved to Jake from the third pew where her grandmother liked to sit. Rachel's grandmother, Esther, turned when her granddaughter did and waved her bejeweled fingers at me. Her blue satin dress would have been more appropriate at a formal wedding than a normal Sunday, but I smiled and waved back.

I liked Esther; she was the epitome of the family matriarch. Even though Rachel could have come to church with us today then sat with her grandma, Esther always insisted that Rachel and her parents accompany her every third Sunday. After church, they'd all go out to whatever restaurant Esther requested then spend the rest of the afternoon at her house, no doubt watching whatever supernatural beast or haunting show was her latest favorite. Rachel complained, but I think she secretly enjoyed her time with Esther, who'd passed on her love of jewelry and fashion to her only grandchild. From her gaudy rings to her eccentric dress, Esther was quirky and lively if not gullibly superstitious, and she loved Rachel more than anybody. I've often wondered if Rachel had been a boy if the compulsory Sunday dinners would exist.

I watched the little ones skip and hop from the doors behind the pulpit and baptistry, bright eyes searching for parents already seated and carrying their construction paper leaves with bible verses printed in their wobbly handwriting. I remembered the craft lessons I used to proudly shove at Mom, every snip of the scissors perfect without a single stray crayon mark, and I made certain to point out how much neater it was than Jake's glue-smeared mess, but she always smiled just as excitedly at his efforts as she had at mine.

One blonde bundle of crumbs and marker-stained fingers leapt into the arms of Coach Bart Joseph. He hugged the boy close before examining the card he'd made in Sunday school. Coach Joseph was the head coach of Jake's football team. To most people, he appeared to be a jolly giant, who stood at around six and a half feet tall with a close-cut dark beard and graying chestnut hair, but Jake's locker-room stories told a different tale.

Coach Joseph had a temper he reserved for his team, and he didn't hesitate to yell his displeasure when they weren't playing well. I'd seen a shadow of that temper three weeks ago during

AP US history. Coach Joseph hated the stereotypical belief that coaches don't make good teachers, and he put a lot of effort into his classes, but when a sophomore corrected him on a date during a discussion of the Declaration of Independence, Coach kind of lost it. The kid was wrong, but that didn't excuse the tirade Coach threw, screaming at the poor, sputtering boy until I thought he'd cry--the boy not Coach. Later, I saw Coach talking to the boy in the hall, apologizing I assume.

As the preacher moved behind the podium, I looked around at all these people, my neighbors, my friends, my teachers. I held the chain out away from my chest and absently ran the pendant across the taut metal. If Coach Joseph had two sides, did everyone? Did all these Sunday smiles hide more?

CHAPTER 6

"I'm starvin'!" Jake yelled as soon as we walked through the foyer, and the smell of roasted pork and potatoes filled my nose. He'd been grumbling through preaching about not having eaten since last night, so without hesitation, he headed to the kitchen. Mom hadn't cooked breakfast because she woke up later than usual, and Jake had decided he'd perish before we could make it back home.

"You stay out of that crock pot, Jacob!" Mom called. "You can snack on some fruit or something till I'm finished with it."

"I'm going upstairs to change," I said, heading up while Mom rushed to keep Jake out of the food, and Dad headed to the family room.

As I plodded toward my room, I thought about the music from my jewelry box. I knew I'd heard it, the porcelain couple tiptoeing in their never-ending dance. Closing the door behind me, I went straight to the box and turned the key, but the couple didn't move. Closing the lid, I picked up the box and examined the underside as though I could see through the cloth and wood to the mechanism. I gave it a little shake before setting it back down with a shrug. Stranger things had happened, I guess—just never to me.

The red and blue lettering on the front of the ACT prep book caught my attention, and I was relieved that Ms. Jordan was offering a prep class. I'd gone about as far as I could on my own, and admittedly science was my weakest area on the practice tests. Just the confidence of having advanced study with her would surely boost my score.

Sitting on the edge of the bed, I pulled off my boots and

tights before yanking off my tunic. The pendant caught on the collar of the tunic and scraped against my lip. "Dang!" I touched my lip, then stared at the tiny smear of blood on the tip of my middle finger. Going to my mirror, I leaned close and brushed the wisps of hair out of my face. Sure enough, a crimson bubble blossomed on my lip, and blood smudged the sparkle of the opal in the pendant's center. Licking my lip, I reached for a tissue from my bedside table drawer and held it to my lip, pulling it back occasionally to see if the blood had stopped. Before tossing the tissue away, I wiped the pendant, and goosebumps tiptoed down my arms. This thing had creeped me out since I got it, and now it'd drawn blood?

I reached up to unfasten the clasp, but each time I thought I'd engaged the clasp's spring, the chain stayed fastened. A wave of complete, unjustified urgency rushed into my gut. I tugged the chain and twisted it around so that I could see the clasp if I tucked my chin in tight and closed one eye. I stepped close to the mirror again.

"Honey, lunch is ready." Mom knocked on my door.

"Mom, come in. I need your help." I grabbed a t-shirt and pulled it over my head just as Mom stepped inside. She was wearing her "I cook to stop the voices in my head" apron over the light blue sweater she'd worn to church. "I can't get this stupid necklace off."

Her eyes were large at my tone. "I thought you liked this necklace."

"*You* like this necklace," I said, grabbing my black yoga pants from a drawer. With Mom in the room, the urgency had diminished, and I felt a little dumb. It was just a necklace, not something out to get me.

After pulling on the pants, I turned and lifted my hair, watching in the mirror as Mom turned the chain until she could reach the clasp. She tilted her head as her brows knitted. I could tell her fingers were working the chain, but it wasn't moving. Finally, she sighed.

"You've sprung the clasp. It won't open. Did you yank on it?" Her eyes met mine in the mirror.

"Well, I might have..." I trailed off, not wanting to admit how ridiculous I felt for freaking out. She swatted my behind, and I twirled in place like my tiny dancers to face her. "Hey! What was that for?" I rubbed my stinging cheek.

"For almost breaking a beautiful antique." She pointed her finger. "You leave it alone, and as soon as I can, I'll take you by Bartholomew's Jewelry and have it properly removed and repaired." She fanned her fingers at my chest. "Besides, it looks so pretty. What would it hurt to just wear it?"

I couldn't tell her it sort of creeped me out. I couldn't admit that I was scared of a necklace, so I just shrugged.

She shook her head. "All that vocabulary, and you have nothing to say?" She patted my cheek and smiled. "Well, come on down to lunch."

"But—" I tugged at the necklace, and she tilted her chin toward her chest, raising one brow as though to say "don't you dare."

"Lunch, now." She turned and walked out, leaving me staring at my reflection.

****

An afternoon spent thumbing through my prep books and reading *Jane Eyre* for AP Literature had left my head aching and my eyes bleary. I pulled off my shirt and pants and slipped into a soft, long nightshirt. After brushing my teeth and washing my face, I pulled back my comforter and slipped between my lilac sheets. But when I laid down, the necklace tightened around my throat. I'd managed to ignore it most of the day while I studied, but now that I had nothing to distract me, the weight of it seemed to press against me. I yanked it none too gently before remembering Mom's glare when she thought I'd tried to break it. We'd go by the jewelry store tomorrow after school, and I'd be rid of it. I could toss it back in my jewelry box and forget about it forever.

****

Blue, blue as the Caribbean, blue as the center of an iceberg, blue as the flames on the kitchen stove.

Her eyes draw me in. It's all I can see, those blue eyes with pupils so small they're almost nonexistent. I try to pull away from her, see more than the eyes, the dark fringe of lashes, but I'm held by something forceful around my arms. I try to look down, to find what is holding me, but there is only black, absolute darkness.

"Ria." The voice belongs to the eyes, no mouth, no face, just the blue of the eyes. "Free me, Ria."

****

I sat up, gasping, searching for blue eyes in the shadows of my room. I closed my eyes, trying to see the dream again. The voice was already fading, but I was certain it was female. What had she said? She'd called me by name. A young voice, a girl, and the eyes—those eyes were so vivid, so bright. She was desperate, the kind of desperation that eats at a person. She wanted something, but what?

Breathing deeply to steady my whole-body shake, I absently reached for the pendant that was hanging backwards around my neck. I stroked the pendant, remembering the sharp pain it had given me earlier, and again, a chill danced up my arms. My brain rationalized that the weird dream came from my own unreasonable fears this afternoon. I scared myself when I couldn't get the necklace off, and the dream had come from that—just like when I watched that creepy clown movie a few months ago then couldn't sleep for two nights. That was all it was, a dream that I'd created myself from making such a big deal out of a stupid necklace.

Dropping the chain, I picked up my phone and pushed the home button. 3:22 AM. Great, maybe I could get a few more hours of sleep, but before I could put the phone back onto my nightstand, it buzzed. A tiny envelope popped up in the left corner of the screen. Something about the innocuous icon made my heart skip. A message wasn't unusual; even an early morning message didn't normally trigger any response other than annoyance. But with those dream eyes still fresh, my unease returned full force. With an unsteady hand, I clicked the message open. No sender number appeared in the spot where a name or number normally popped up. My eyes skipped to the bottom, and I dropped the phone on the bed. "Free me, Ria" stared up at me.

CHAPTER 7

Dawn found me still staring at my phone, but the message remained the same. I tucked my legs tightly against my chest. Each time I read the message, it brought the dream back in living color. Blue eyes, darkness, and that voice. As soon as I'd seen the message, I remembered her words. "Free me, Ria." Swallowing past the dryness in my throat, I pushed the home button on my screen.

What was going on? It had to be some sick joke, but who would send me a message that just happened to also appear in my dream? How was that even possible? At first, I thought maybe I was still dreaming, one of those dreams where you only think you're awake, but every time I opened the message, there it was. With no number, I had no way of knowing who sent it.

When my alarm blasted into the silence of my room, I jumped and quickly found the button on the back of the clock to stop the blaring. I scrubbed my hands over my face. The idea of facing the day made my stomach turn. I'd show it to Mom and tell her about my dream. Her inevitable eye roll and "it's nothing" would settle me. Her rationale would agree with what my brain said was impossible, and everything would feel normal again. Nodding with resolve, I grabbed clean underwear and headed to the bathroom.

****

I dropped my messenger bag on the island in the kitchen while Mom poured me a cup of coffee. Glancing out the French doors, I noticed that the dreary weather perfectly matched my mood, and I didn't smile when Mom passed me the cup. Now that I was dressed and downstairs, my nightmare seemed far away and my fear even more ridiculous. She raised an eyebrow as she tightened the belt of her fuzzy, yellow robe.

"You okay, honey?" she asked, tucking behind her ear a strand of hair that had escaped her sloppy ponytail. The store didn't open for another two hours, so Mom had likely not showered yet. "You look tired. Have a bad night?"

Taking a deep breath, I reached into my bag for my phone. "Sort of. I had this creepy dream, and then I got a weird message right after that."

She moved back to the coffee pot and filled the mug sitting beside it. "Tell me about your dream."

"There were eyes, really blue eyes and a voice, like a girl's voice. She wanted me to free her, then I got this message." I clicked my home button and opened my messages. The message should have been right on top, but it wasn't. I scrolled through my message home screen, all the way to the bottom then back up to the top, but the message was gone. My heart pounded. What the crap? Where was it?

Mom leaned over the island to peek at my phone. "What message?"

"It was here! I—I saw it! I stared at it for like three hours." I scrolled again. "It was right here." When I looked up, she moved around the island to stand next to me.

"Maybe you accidentally deleted it?"

"No, no, it was there before I took a shower." I shook my head and glanced around the kitchen, as though the message were hiding in a corner behind the potted plants.

"Well, what did it say?" She tilted her head to force me to look at her.

I ran my hand across my forehead, knowing that what I was about to say was exactly what I didn't want to say without

55

the evidence that the message would have brought. "It said the same thing the girl said in the dream, 'Free me, Ria.' "

"The message said the same thing as the person in your dream? How is that possible, honey? Are you sure you were awake? Could it have been part of your dream?" She pressed her hand against my cheek, then leaned in to touch her lips to my forehead in typical Mom fashion to check for a fever. "Maybe you should go back to bed for a few hours. You've been studying awfully hard lately."

I pulled away, then shoved my phone back in the bag. "I'm fine. It's nothing." Great, now I was comforting myself. "I need to go today."

Her gentle smile made the corners of her eyes crinkle. "You always say that. It's okay to take a mental health day occasionally."

"Ms. Jordan is having the first study group after school. I told her I'd be there."

She shook her head and touched my hand where it gripped my messenger bag strap. "Okay, but if you need to come home, text me, and I'll pick you up. Oh, what about the necklace?" She flicked her fingers at the pendant still stuck around my neck against my green sweater.

I touched the stone, which felt warm. I wanted it off, but the study group meeting was more important. I hadn't thought of the time conflict until right that minute. Besides, giving in to some dumb, childish fear would only make me feel even more ridiculous. "I guess it'll have to wait till tomorrow." I walked into the foyer and called for Jake as Mom followed me out of the kitchen with a covered Styrofoam cup of coffee and a package of toaster pastries. Just like every morning, Jake ran downstairs, hair wet and mussed, as he tugged on a sweatshirt. When he reached the bottom, he yanked on his tennis shoes, which were habitually untied, and turned back to take his breakfast before depositing a reluctant, quick kiss to the cheek Mom turned toward him.

"Where's your bag, Jacob?" Mom asked.

He tore open the silver wrapping of the pastries and shoved in half of one, spewing chocolate crumbs as he answered, "In the truck."

She shook her head and smiled. "Have a good day, you two. Text me, Miriam."

I nodded as Jake opened the door and looked back at her retreating form. "Text her about what?"

"Nothing. She thinks I need a day off." I walked to the truck but kept quiet about the dream and the mystery text. No way I was sharing that with my brother. He'd tease me relentlessly if he knew.

He opened the door and slid in, looking at me as if I'd grown another head. "And you didn't take it? All that studying is making your brain soft."

I sighed and crossed my arms. "Just start the truck."

As he cranked the key and set his cup in the console, he laughed. "Mom offers you a day off and you don't take it? Dang, you must be adopted 'cause there is no way we can be related."

"Of yeah, and if she'd offered to let you take the day off, would you?" I already knew the answer. With football in full swing, Jake would never miss a day of practice, but I couldn't pass up the chance to point this out.

He gave me a quick, slanted gaze as he turned to back out of the driveway. "Yeah, but that's different. I got practice. You've just got—" he shrugged "—whatever it is you do during the day."

As he shifted the truck into gear, I rolled my eyes. There was no point trying to explain to Jake—again—why school was so important to me. He'd never understand why I needed to be good at something. I couldn't have sports like him, but I could have education. I needed it, needed it as much as he needed the cheering crowds. It kept me centered, knowing I was in control of my grades. Of course teachers played a role in that, but I never had a problem impressing any of them. Teachers loved hard work, and usually they rewarded it.

"Speaking of practice," he said, "it may be a late one tonight. We've got Bethel Christian Friday night, and we gotta learn some new plays."

"I'll be in study group this afternoon so that works out for me."

When Jake's phone dinged, he reached for his back pocket and grinned as he looked at the screen.

"Eyes on the road. I didn't dress for an accident this morning." I scowled as he dropped the phone in the empty cup holder beside his coffee.

"I can't help it your friend is trying to text me this early in the morning."

"That was Rachel? She texted you? What did she say?" When I reached for his phone, he swatted at my hand and tucked the phone inside his hoodie pocket.

"Relax, she just told me to have a good day." His grin didn't feel conciliatory. He hummed as he took a sip of coffee.

Great. First a crazy dream then a weird text and now my best friend texting my hoochie brother. This was going to be an awesome day.

CHAPTER 8

I massaged the crease that had set up permanent residence between my brows. My head had hurt since lunch, probably from being awake since before dawn, and despite the three ibuprofen I'd sneaked from my bag, it lingered. Though the last bell of the day had rung about ten minutes ago, I knew I still had to make it through Ms. Jordan's study session. I rubbed my temples, hoping to ease the tension there, as a few stranglers slipped into the room. Most of the seats were full, and I was forced to the back row even though I'd gotten to her room almost immediately after the bell. I guessed a lot of people needed this session.

"You okay?" a voice from beside me asked.

I dropped my hands, a little embarrassed to have attracted anyone's pity. "Just a headache." I turned toward the girl who'd just sat down across from me. Her short, dark hair curled around her ears, and her bright azure eyes seemed almost too large for her tiny face. She was cute in a pixie kind of way. I'd never seen her before, but her friendly smile brought out one of my own. "Not exactly the best thing for an after-school study group."

Her smile broadened. "I know what you mean. I can think of a million other things I'd rather be doing." She laid her notebook on the desk. "You weren't saving this seat, were you?"

I shook my head but answered anyway. "No, I couldn't convince any of my friends they needed this." I gestured toward the front of the room.

"I know, right! My friends bailed on me, too." As she sat, she tugged her mod-style dress over her knees. The brown and orange color blocking matched the brown boots covering her calves and her cream cardigan. "I'm Dee," she said, bringing her left hand to her chest. The light shined off her gold-tone watch and bracelet.

"Hi, I'm Ria." I extended my right hand, a gesture my dad had embedded into me since childhood. But Dee shrank away even though we were separated by a foot of tile, a distressed look briefly crossing her face.

Her nose wrinkled, not quite in disgust but close to it. "Sorry, I kinda have a thing about germs—not to say you're germy! I just—"

I smiled again. "It's okay. My cousin is the same way. I understand."

Her relief showed in her easy smile. "Thanks, most people get all worked up about it."

"I like your outfit. Those boots are fantastic."

"Thanks," she said again, smoothing her cardigan. "It's vintage. I love old things. Speaking of which, your necklace is beautiful."

I touched the pendant. I'd forgotten I was even wearing it. "Thank you, it was a gift. But how did you know it's old?"

She winked. "I can just tell. Vintage is my favorite thing."

Before I could respond, Ms. Jordan walked in, screwing the lid on a barely touched cola bottle. "Welcome! I didn't expect so many of you! Well, let's get started."

I smiled one last time at Dee, then turned to face forward. From the corner of my eye, I could see Dee. Her smile widened as she still watched me before finally turning toward Ms. Jordan.

****

An hour later, Ms. Jordan erased the wipe board and sighed. "Okay, everyone, I think that's enough for one day. We'll meet again on Wednesday. If you can't be here, that's fine. Make the meetings you can." She moved the thick ACT prep book to her desk before looking up with raised brows. "What are you waiting for? Go." She smiled and made a shooing motion with her hands.

I glanced over at Dee while I closed my notebook. She was capping her pen and gathering her notebook. "It was nice to meet you. Will you be back on Wednesday?"

"Yeah, I need all the help I can get." She stood and pulled at her cardigan before arranging her things in her arms.

"I haven't seen you around. Are you new?" I fell into step beside her as the others filed out.

"No, I've been around. I've seen you a few times. I'm a senior, so we don't really have any classes together." Her eyes dropped to her watch. "I hate to be rude, but I've gotta go. I'll see you Wednesday."

Ms. Jordan's voice caused me to turn toward the front of the room where she was packing her overlarge, quilted bag. "Thanks for coming, Ria. I'll see you next time."

"Thanks, Ms. Jordan." I turned to tell Dee goodbye, but she was already gone.

CHAPTER 9

I'd just about reached my tolerance for *Jane Eyre* when Jake stuck his head in my door.

"Rachel wanted me to see if you're going to the game Friday night." He shoved a chocolate chip cookie into his mouth before brushing crumbs from his t-shirt into my bedroom floor.

My brows dipped. "She texted *you* to ask if *I* wanted to go to the game? Why didn't she just text me?" I grabbed my phone from the table next to my bed and checked the screen. Sure enough, I had no recent texts.

Jake shrugged. "Don't know. You goin' or what?" He braced his hands on either side of my door frame.

"I haven't thought about it. Is it an important game?" I set *Jane Eyre* on my table.

"Dang, Ria, don't you notice anything besides school work? We play Bethel, remember? They almost beat us last time." At my blank expression, Jake rolled his gray eyes. "Yes, it's an important game." A grin lit his face. "And Rachel and I are going out to eat after it's over."

I opened my mouth to protest, but he held up his hand. "It's a burger and fries, not a marriage proposal. I told you, I kinda like her. Stop worrying."

"Uh huh." I narrowed my eyes. "Just remember we sleep in the same house, and I'm smarter than you." I put up two fingers and swung them between my eyes and his. "I'm watching you."

Jake laughed, tossing his brown curls back from his forehead. "Okay, sis, I hear ya, but you can't control everything. Text her when you figure out if you're going." He turned to leave.

My notebook caught my attention, and I remembered Dee.

I had forgotten to ask him about her Monday night. "Hey, do you know a girl named Dee? She's a senior that I met at study group yesterday afternoon."

Jake leaned back into my bedroom but shook his head. "What's she look like? I might have seen her."

"Short dark hair, real tiny girl, great fashion sense."

Jake smirked. "Yeah, whatever that means. None of that rings a bell. Maybe she's new."

"She said she'd been here awhile." I shrugged. "She's really cute. Maybe I could introduce you two." I raised my brows.

He cocked his head and frowned. "Nice try. I'm still takin' out Rachel."

"It was worth a shot," I called as he started down the hall.

Sighing, I shoved all my books but *Jane Eyre* into my messenger bag. I still needed to read at least ten more pages before bed, but a shower sounded amazing. After closing my door, I stripped out of my clothes and headed to the bathroom. I adjusted the water and stepped in, wetting my hair and savoring the warm water over my tense shoulders. I shampooed and conditioned my hair, then picked up the soap. When I ran it across my chest, it bumped the necklace I still wore. I'd forgotten to ask Mom about taking me by the jewelry shop to have it removed. I guessed it wasn't really hurting anything. I mean, I'd forgotten it was there, and Dee had complimented it. She clearly knew her stuff, so maybe I'd keep it on after all. Yesterday's irrational fear seemed far away and really stupid. It was a pretty necklace, not a pentagram cursed by a wicked witch in some movie.

When I finished, I stepped out, dried, and went back into my bedroom for some clean night clothes, then dried my hair so it wouldn't be too crazy tomorrow. I slipped into bed and grabbed my novel. Ten more pages. I started to read, but my eyes kept slipping closed. I straightened in the bed and rearranged the pillows, trying for a less comfortable position. I tried to focus on the horrible scream Jane heard echoing through the house, but my eyes refused to stay open, and when they slid closed again, I let the book drop.

****

The room is dark. Weak moonlight shines through a tiny window high on the cement-block wall, but it does little to chase the shadows from the corners. The ground is level with the window, making me think I'm in a basement. I try to stand, but the pain in my ankle brings me back to my knees. I crawl to the rectangle of light on the concrete floor. My heaving chest is only partially from the pain shooting up my leg. I'm scared, terrified, of someone.

I slide on my butt until my back is pressed against the cool wall. Something scuttles in the darkness, and I swing my eyes to the door. It looks like it's made of metal, painted dark but chipped near the handle. It's not the typical knob; it's heavy, the kind you push down to open. To the right is an enormous black iron boiler with pipes leading up into the ceiling.

More scurrying, closer this time, causes me to quickly draw my legs to my chest. The pain makes me wince. My polyester dress is rough against my skin. The light pink is covered in dust, and I rub at the spots while tears fill my eyes. "Mother will be so upset." The voice is in my head although I don't recognize it. I glance at my watch. It's gold with tiny stones gleaming where the numbers should be. "They'll be gone soon."

Male voices come from down the hall, laughing and jeering. I scoot farther into the shadows, praying they will not open the door. "Check in there," one voice says.

A higher, shriller female voice squeals in delight. "Come out, come out, wherever you are!"

Then the door handle screeches, and the door scrapes against the floor as it pushes in, flooding the dinginess with light. The light behind the figure keeps me from seeing any features, but the boy laughs and says to me, "It's about time." He calls over his shoulder, "I found her."

****

Gasping, I sprang up in bed, my eyes scanning the room for my would-be attacker. Sweat trickled down my back and peppered my forehead. I looked down for the soiled pink polyester dress but saw only my nightgown. To my left, my lamp still burned familiarly, mocking the slamming of my heart. No cement blocks or metal doors, just my room.

I closed my eyes and took a deep breath or two to settle the staccato pounding. The dream had been so real, so frightening.

When I opened my eyes, I saw *Jane Eyre* where it had landed on the floor beside me. Stupid Gothic novel had clearly done its work and left me with a nightmare. My lit teacher would crap herself with excitement if I told her. Picking it up, I took it to my bag. No more reading tonight.

It had felt so real, as if I weren't just making it up but like I'd actually lived it. It felt like a memory, not a creation. But that's not possible. I had no idea where the dream even occurred, much less why I was being chased or who was chasing me. It was a dream—that's all it could be—a dream caused by too much studying and apparently Victorian hysterics.

But as I turned toward my bed, I caught a glimpse of myself in the mirror, and for a fraction of a second, I didn't recognize my own reflection. The face shape was mine but not. The hair was mine but darker. A shimmer, a glint of something me but not me all at the same time. I focused on my eyes. Crystal blue replaced green, and I heard my dream voice. "Free me, Ria."

CHAPTER 10

I couldn't tell Mom. She'd think I was losing my mind. I ran the straightening iron through the last section of my hair and released the clip I had separating the chunks. Opening the top drawer beneath my bathroom sink, I pulled out my face powder. As I swiped my brush across my nose, I shook my head.

"It was just a dream," I said aloud, hoping to convince the slight tremor in my hand. "It was a dream, and you freaked yourself out." Dropping the powder back in the drawer, I reached for my eyeshadow and brush and stroked my favorite color over my lids before dabbing my lashes with mascara. After slathering on some lip gloss, I pulled my fingers through my hair and tried a smile that quickly turned to a frown.

"Yeah, I don't believe anything you have to say, but you're gonna fake it till you make it." If I couldn't feel normal, I could at least look it. Maybe Mom wouldn't see the dark circles if I seemed in good spirits; no matter how much makeup I wore or how careful I was with my outfit, I was far from okay. But I needed to seem that way.

First the nightmare with the eyes and the weird text, then last night's dream about being pursued and hiding in a basement. A shiver skipped down my arms, and the hair stood on end. I stared at my face a moment longer, almost willing it to transform as it had last night. "No, it didn't. You only think it did because you scared yourself." I sighed. "And now you're talking to yourself." Maybe Mom was right; I'd been studying too hard. I couldn't keep the crease from my brow nor the ache out of my head.

I avoided the full-length mirror in my room as I grabbed my messenger bag and adjusted it over my shoulder. I yanked my covers up my bed and smoothed them before walking out of the room, where I nearly ran into Jake. A glance at my watch told me he was early—for him anyway.

"I'm starvin' this morning," he said, pulling a blue Florida Gators sweatshirt over his head.

"When are you not?" I asked, as he dropped his arm around my shoulders. I raised a brow as I looked pointedly at his arm. "What're you doing?"

"Can't I just show my little sister some love?" He squeezed my shoulder.

"Ew, not without questions." I pushed his hand off, then something occurred to me, and I stopped in the middle of the hallway. "It's Rachel, isn't it? What did you do?"

Jake kept walking, whistling as he took the stairs two at a time. I raced after him and skidded into his back as he entered the kitchen.

"Miriam! Slow down," Mom said, as she placed two mugs on the island.

"Mom, something happened with Rachel. Make him tell me what's going on." I knew I sounded totally whiny, but Jake was up to something. I put both my fists on my hips.

Mom looked up as Dad entered and went to her, dropping a kiss on her upturned lips. "What's going on about what?" Dad asked, moving toward the coffee pot.

By this time, Jake had taken a mixing bowl from the cabinet and half-filled it with Fruity Rolls cereal and milk. He shoveled a heaping spoonful into his mouth, then said, "She doesn't think I should be in a good mood."

Mom pursed her lips at Jake. "Don't talk with your mouth full, and I doubt that's what's wrong with her."

"He's dating Rachel, and something happened. He's being too nice to me this morning." I took my mug from the island

and sipped, giving Jake the stink eye over the rim.

"I thought you wanted him to ask her out," Dad said, munching on some grapes he grabbed from the fridge.

"Exactly!" Jake swallowed his cereal. "Women! You can't please 'em, right, Dad?"

Dad lifted his mug toward Jake and started to nod his head, before Mom reached up and gently tugged his ear.

"Did you do something to her?" I asked again.

Jake smirked like a cat that had swallowed the canary. "A gentleman doesn't kiss and tell."

"Mom!" I turned to Mom as she covered a smile behind her hand. My throat felt tight, like I might cry. I never cry. What was wrong with me? I faced the cabinets and pretended to put more sweetener in my mug so no one would see. I must be more tired than I had thought, or maybe it was hormones. Almost crying about Rachel and Jake? The dream rushed back to me, and my throat tightened even more as did the tension in my neck and head.

The sweetener ruse must not have fooled Mom because she stepped closer to me and put her hand on my back as she tilted her head to get a better look at my face. "You okay?" she whispered.

I blinked rapidly to force away the tears and turned to her. "I don't want him to hurt her feelings."

Mom sighed. "Jake, did you do something to upset Rachel?"

Jake put his bowl in the sink. "No, I didn't. I'm just in a good mood." He pulled his phone from his pocket and looked at the screen. He leaned against the counter beside me, facing me so that I could see him. "I like her, okay? We like each other. She makes me...smile." He grinned like he did when he was nine and had made me laugh with some silly joke. "So stop worryin' it's all good. You can't control everything, sis." Hadn't he said the same thing last night? Was that what people thought, that I needed to control everything? I started to internally deny it but then decided he was probably right. I did try to control things. If I could control a situation, I wouldn't be disappointed.

I dropped my gaze back to my mug and tried to breathe deeply to clear my eyes. I felt Mom's eyes on me again, analyzing. She rubbed small circles in the center of my back.

"Go get your stuff, son," Mom said. A sideways look told me she was motioning Dad out of the kitchen. I heard his steps, then she moved in front of me and took my mug, setting it on the counter. "Now, young lady, you're going to tell me what's really going on with you. Look at me please."

I cleared my throat, trying to fake her out, but there was no fooling Mom. So I fanned my eyes to dry the tears before they ruined my makeup. "I think I'm tired. I didn't sleep well."

"Again? Maybe it's time for that day off." She pushed my hair over my left shoulder.

"I can't. I have study group after school again today."

"It wouldn't hurt to skip one day, honey. I'll call the girls at the shop and tell them—"

But I shook my head again. "No, I'm fine. I'll rest this weekend. I promise." I wanted a normal school day. I needed it.

She straightened the pendant where it lay on my black blouse and sighed. "You know we're proud of you. You don't have to keep up this pace."

My half-hearted smile felt artificial, even to me. "I know. I want to raise my ACT score three more points at least. If I can do that, then I can relax."

She twisted her mouth to the side, her brows creating a deep crease, as if she could see inside my head. "You *will* rest this weekend. I mean it. No work."

I nodded. "Yes, ma'am." But as soon as I said it, I saw the dark silhouette of the dream boy and heard his taunting voice, *"I found her."* And I knew I was lying.

CHAPTER 11

I pulled my US history book from my locker and shoved it into my messenger bag. When I closed the door, Rachel's smiling face made me jump. "Geez!" My hand flew to my chest where my heart hammered. "Dang, you scared the crap out of me!"

Rachel's smile only widened. "Sorry, I thought you saw me come up." Her black hair, charcoal sweater, and pink scarf were perfect as usual. She was carrying her history book as well. "Did you get your history terms finished?"

I could tell by the way she raised her brows that she didn't finish hers. "Not yet, but we have till Friday."

"I haven't seen you much this week. Wanna get together after school and work on them?" Her diamond hoops jiggled as she tilted her head to look at me, and we started walking toward Coach Joseph's room.

"Can't. I have Ms. Jordan's study group after school. I was actually going to ask you if you wanted to go."

Rachel twirled a lock of hair around her index finger and looked down at her black flats. "Well, I uh, sorta thought, maybe—"

"You want to come over later to see Jake," I said with a sigh. I loved Rachel, and as scared as I was that Jake might not be serious about her, I wanted her to be happy, and I knew, at least right now, that he made her happy. "He won't be out of practice till closer to 5:00. He's going to give me a ride after the study session. You want to wait and ride home with us?"

Her smile was so wide I thought her face would split. "Yes!"

"So you'll go to the study session?" I stopped in front of Coach's door, the outside sporting a laminated poster of George

Washington crossing the Delaware River.

She screwed up her tiny nose as if she had smelled Cain's latest pile. "Are you gonna be mad if I say no? I get enough of Ms. Jordan in chemistry."

"I thought you liked her." I turned the handle as the tardy bell began to ring.

"I do, but Jake said I could watch him practice if I wanted, and if it's the choice between Ms. Jordan and him…" Rachel sighed deeply, a dreamy look on her face. "I choose him."

I rolled my eyes just as Coach boomed from his podium at the front, "It's about time, ladies."

"Sorry, Coach. The bell was sorta still ringing when we walked in, so technically, can we be *not* tardy?" Rachel whined, but I barely heard her pleading for leniency because his words took me back to the night before. A boy silhouetted by too bright hall lights. A boy who pushed open a heavy metal door. A boy who found me sitting among the mice, hiding in the dark. The boy in my dream had said almost the exact same thing. But it wasn't just the words. The voice in my dream was the same.

CHAPTER 12

Rachel tugged me forward. Coach shook his head and waved us to our seats, but it all happened in slow-motion, my thoughts too wrapped up in what couldn't be true. Coach Joseph could *not* be the boy from the dream. Why would I dream about Coach? The dream had felt so real, like I'd lived it, not thought it up, but Coach had to be in his forties. It wasn't even logical. It didn't have to be if it was only a dream, but what if it wasn't? What if it was more?

And why did it feel like it was a memory and not a dream?

I sat mechanically and rubbed the incessant pounding between my eyes. Sitting across from me, Rachel pulled her notebook toward her and opened it to a fresh page before clicking her pen, poised to take notes like we did every day. I looked around the room at all the other kids, most doing the same, but I left my notebook closed and concentrated on Coach's face and voice. He was lecturing about Gettysburg, but my mind was in a battle of its own.

I studied him harder than I've ever studied for one of his tests. His height set him apart from many people. I closed my eyes and tried to see the boy from the dream. Yes, he seemed tall, filling the space created by the open door, but I was sitting, so he would have seemed tall regardless. The tension in my gritted jaw only added to the throbbing in my temples, but I had to remember as many details as possible. His hair was mostly dark now, so it would be even more so then. Did the dream boy have dark hair? He would have been a jock. Did the dream boy look like a jock? The harder I tried to summon a full picture, the less I seemed sure of and the more my head ached.

"Miss Gabriel, am I boring you?"

I jerked and opened my eyes to see Coach with his forearms braced against his podium and his eyes boring holes through me. "No, sir, I—"my palms began to sweat at being called out "—I just have a bad headache."

"Do you need to go to the nurse?" He walked around the podium. I stared at him in his jeans and black polo-style shirt, and I remembered his son rushing into his arms at church. He looked harmless, a dad from a TV commercial. I was trying to imagine him without the beard and the years lining his eyes, imagine him as the monster chasing a frightened girl.

I shook my head, but the voice in my head whispered, "Free me, Ria." My face heated, my hands tingled, as my pulse sped up as it had in the dream.

Rachel touched my shoulder. She leaned across the aisle, concern marking her face. "Are you okay?"

I nodded blankly but words failed me. I couldn't seem to catch my breath, and my chest tightened. Coach walked down the aisle toward me.

"You need to go to the nurse." He reached out his big hand, but I shrank back, clutching my arms in to keep him from touching me. Panic gripped me, screaming not to let him near me. I scrambled up and back, bumping into the edge of the desk behind me. Every set of eyes watched me, and my fear soared. The dream voice screamed at me. "Get out of this room."

Coach looked at Rachel. "Go with her."

But I was already at the door.

CHAPTER 13

When I stepped out, I plopped onto the metal bench beside Coach's door, leaning my head back against the wall behind me. The tingling in my hands subsided, and my breath came back. But the door swung open, and Rachel stepped into the hall.

"You okay? What happened?" She leaned toward me and put her hand on my shoulder.

How could I explain what had just happened without sounding completely mental? Even my best friend would think I was losing it if I told her that I thought Coach Joseph had tormented me in a dream where I wasn't actually myself and had the voice of some other girl. Yeah, not going to happen. "I'm …I don't know …I got lightheaded I guess." I rubbed my forehead against the ache that was quickly becoming my constant companion.

"Coach told me to make sure you got to the nurse's office." She took my hand from my face and tugged gently. But I shook my head.

"I'm fine. I just need a minute."

Rachel's brows rose. "Are you sure? I really think you should go."

I hadn't been to the nurse's office since coming to high school. I always kept any medicine I might need in my bag even though the rules forbade it. I only knew where the office was because I'd walked past it going to different classes. But the thought of going back into Coach's room was less than appealing, and my ibuprofen was in my bag at my desk.

"What would it hurt?" Rachel asked with a shrug. "You can lie around on her couch for the rest of the hour. You know I'll take notes, and you can copy them later."

That sounded a lot better than facing Coach and my nightmare again. "Yeah, you're right." I pushed myself up from the bench. "But you go on back inside. Maybe he'll give the definition to one of those terms and save us a little work." I tried to smile to reassure her, but it came off half-heartedly at best. I didn't want to explain my freak out to her, and I knew she'd ask again if we were alone in the nurse's office. At Rachel's nod, I started down the hall.

When I arrived at the office, the door was open. The room was small with a curtained area in one corner that I assumed was the exam table, though I didn't know who or what the nurse might be examining. As far as I could tell, she basically doled out antacids and cough drops if you were lucky. Having a nurse in high school was pointless. When we were little and a scraped knee could happen at basically any time, the nurse offered much-needed Band-Aids and suckers to make the hurt stop, but now? Not so much, and most of the kids just went to her office to get out of class.

I glanced around. No wonder students hardly saw her in the halls. I'd spend my whole day in here, too. The navy blue rug matched the fluffy throw pillows on the black pleather couch which was flanked by end tables on which glowed dove-gray lamps. Opposite the couch sat an oversized pleather chair with an ottoman. With the framed beach scenes, the room looked more like a cozy living room.

"Hello?" I stepped farther into the space as the blue and gray curtain swished along its curved rod. Phoebe Tadmor, a middle-aged woman with bottle blonde hair, stood beside a mirrored medicine cabinet above a small sink. Her hot-pink top and striped leggings would have looked fantastic on Rachel, but on this woman, they seemed like a tragic attempt at youth. Her bangles jingled as she snapped shut a compact in her hand

and raised a disdaining brow at me.

"Yes?" she asked with tilt of her head that made me feel as though I'd just interrupted an important medical diagnosis instead of beauty hour.

It was then I realized I didn't really know what to say. "Um, Coach Joseph sent me down here." I fiddled with my hands, popping my fingers nervously. "I have a headache."

That lofty brow of hers turned into a full-fledged sneer, and her pink-glossed lips puckered, giving way to the wrinkles she seemed desperate to hide. "A headache?"

I nodded as she rolled her eyes and opened the mirrored door of the cabinet and took out a bottle. She pointed to a water cooler partially hidden by the chair and ottoman, and she popped the bottle's lid, shaking one pill from it as I filled a tiny paper cup. She handed me the pill, and I swallowed it before tossing the cup in the can beside the cooler.

"I suppose you want to stay here for a while?" she asked. The hands she put on her hips somehow made her look even more ridiculous in that fluorescent top. After I nodded, she motioned to the couch with a flip of her be-ringed fingers as she retrieved a cell phone from the table closest to the sink. "I'll be back." Her hips swung overtly like the whole football team was watching and she enjoyed it as she stepped out of the room. I could hear her flats clicking down the hall.

I flopped onto the couch, leaned my head back, closed my eyes, and tried to let the solitude of the room soak in. But my mind couldn't rest. None of this seemed logical. My entire life I'd relied on my mind. I was the smart one, the dependable one. Jake had his athletics, and I had my books. If I wanted to know something, I looked it up. If I didn't feel confident, I studied. Now, it felt like my mind was betraying me. Dreams were one thing, alone in my room where no one could see, but school was my safety blanket. How had the dreams invaded the one place I should have been in control?

The dream boy's image shot into my mind, only this time he had Coach's face. I tried to shake the image from my head, but the sound of kids laughing as they walked toward the door jerked me up. I turned my head away so that they couldn't see my face when they passed by the open door. I didn't want anyone—anyone else—to know I was in the nurse's office. It was bad enough that my entire class knew I'd had a meltdown. By the end of the day, it would be all over school that I had some incurable disease and had passed out in the cafeteria face down in the macaroni surprise.

My head throbbed harder. No chance that one pill would wipe it out. I needed to go back to class and take a few more. But the thought of going back had my stomach churning. I glanced at the medicine cabinet and wondered if I could take another couple before Nurse Tadmor returned. Was I actually thinking about swiping pills from the nurse? I closed my eyes and rubbed my temples. Well, wasn't this day just spiraling out of control!

Before I could follow through on my blatant rule breaking, Nurse Tadmor's voice interrupted me. She was on her phone right outside the door. She didn't bother to hide the disdain in her voice as she said, "Oh, I don't know, just some girl who claims to have a headache." She paused, then continued. "You aren't telling me anything I don't already know. They will do anything to get out of class. I mean honestly, as if I don't have enough to do already."

I rolled my eyes. I'd been reduced to the snotty gossip of our pretentious nurse. I gritted my teeth, making the throb in my head increase.

"No, it isn't at all like when we were in school here. You can't trust any of them," she continued. She peeked around the door frame, and I looked back at her with as much venom as her hateful comments. If I weren't so desperate to escape Coach's classroom, I would have marched out of there. I looked at the clock hanging near the exam curtain. Another fifteen minutes. The hour couldn't pass quickly enough.

CHAPTER 14

I waited outside the classroom as the last of the class filed out. I'd shooed Rachel on to her next class, and she hadn't really hesitated as much as I would have liked for her to, then I remembered she had chemistry with Jake, so it didn't sting for long.

When the last two girls stepped out, I went in for my bag and books. I hoped Coach would be too distracted erasing the board or stacking papers to notice me, but I hadn't made it halfway in before he turned and started walking toward me. My heart began to race as though I was training for Olympic sprints, and I gathered my things without looking at him.

"Ria, are you okay? What did the nurse say?" He stopped about two feet from me, and I could feel his eyes on my face as I pulled the strap of my bag over my shoulder.

"She gave me a pill and just let me sit on her couch. I'm fine, sir." I crammed my notebook in the bag without bothering to be gentle. But before I could turn for the door, he touched my shoulder.

I very nearly cried out from the shock that shot down my body. He wasn't rough. In fact, had I not been so keyed up, I doubt I would have even noticed the pressure of it. But with my body betraying me at every turn today, my anxiety was off the charts, and I flinched as if he'd hit me, twisting my shoulder away from him and finally meeting his confused face. Then I felt her, the girl I'd been in my dream, the girl who'd cowered in the dark. She was in my head, glaring through my eyes at Coach Joseph. But she wasn't afraid as she had been last night. She was angry.

"Don't touch me," hissed from my mouth.

He jerked his hand back, his eyes going as round as plates.

"I'm sorry; I didn't mean to upset you." He stepped back and bumped into the arm of a desk, sending it squawking in protest against the tile.

My arm worked of its own accord, slamming my hand on the desk beside me. I was watching myself with no control of my body as I took a step toward him, and he continued to back away. I felt the burning hate radiating from me but couldn't stop it. My eyes narrowed into dangerous slits as my lips sneered in rage, my breath sawing in and out while I shook so hard I knew my teeth would have chattered had I not clenched them. The rushing blood in my head drowned all thought except one: vengeance. *"He needs to suffer, Ria, like he made me suffer."* The whisper belied the fury I felt.

Coach had backed all the way to his own desk at the front. His hands reached out behind him to grip the edge as he watched me with hooded eyes. "Ria, what's wrong with you?"

A step closer. Another. I had no idea what this body I no longer controlled would do when or if I reached him, but relentlessly, I moved forward. When the toes of our shoes nearly touched, his face changed. The beard vanished; the hair became shaggy. The wrinkles from years spent coaching in the summer sun melted. The face staring back became that of his youth. And I knew. I knew without a doubt that when I next saw the dream boy he'd have this face. Coach Joseph's face.

"I see you." Her words came through me again.

Coach's mouth dropped as his brows raised. Voices invaded my cloudy brain, and I turned my head toward the open door. A boy swatted at the face of another boy who ducked, laughing into the room. Other kids followed while the bell began shrieking at tardy students.

The sound seemed to slap me back to myself, and I stumbled back a step and met Coach's eyes briefly before running for the door.

CHAPTER 15

What was wrong with me? It felt like I was losing my mind. I couldn't concentrate in fourth hour physics. I waited the entire hour to be called to the office or the counselor's, something, for my behavior in Coach's room. While Ms. Jordan lectured, I drifted in my thoughts, seeing the dream boy and Coach once again merged and hearing him taunting me—no, not me, the dream girl.

But when I closed my eyes, it wasn't someone else; it was me. I felt the fear of being stalked, hunted in the dark, like some animal. I heard the mice scurrying near me. I saw the light spilling through the open door. It wasn't some unnamed girl. It was me.

When the bell rang, I gathered my things robotically, wondering if it might be best to call Mom and have her pick me up.

"Ria," Ms. Jordan called as I moved toward the door, "will you be at the study session this afternoon?"

My stomach flipped at the thought of an hour after school when I wasn't even certain I could finish the day. "I'm not feeling so great." At the look of concern on her face, I added, "I think I might be getting a cold or something."

The corners of her lips turned down. "I'm sorry to hear that. I'm planning on giving a short practice test today so that we can analyze responses next time."

"So if I miss today, I won't really have anything to go off of next time?" As much as I hated the thought of spending all day at school and then an hour after school, I really hated the idea that I'd be out of the loop for *another* session if I missed today.

I absolutely couldn't let some screwed up dream keep me from doing what I knew needed to be done. This was important. It was reality, not some stupid dream. This would help me feel in control again.

She shrugged. "I'm afraid so."

I nodded. "Okay, I think I can tough it out." I gave a closed-lip smile and walked away. Four hours. Four hours of pretending everything was normal. I could do that. I hoped.

****

The day had taken a huge toll on me. Apparently, 'normal' was harder than I had thought it would be. I hadn't been called to the office, and I'd managed to fight through my headache, but I didn't know what tomorrow in Coach's class might bring. I couldn't think past surviving the afternoon.

I was completely wiped, and Ms. Jordan was late. I'd only stayed to take this stupid test, and she was taking her sweet time. I knew my score on the test I was waiting to take would be terrible, but I had to take it so that I wouldn't be behind. I folded my arms and put my head down on my hands.

My phone buzzed. I groaned as I raised my head and pulled it from my bag. Rachel was texting, telling me she would see me as soon as Jake's practice was over. I was about to text back when Dee came into the room through the back door. As before, she was dressed impeccably in a vintage 80s blue jean skirt with a tight yoke at the top and two ruffles at the bottom and a loose, pink sweater that draped off of one her thin shoulders. Tucking her short black curls behind her left ear, she sat and smiled.

"Hey, I was hoping you'd be here." Her bright blue eyes landed on my phone, and I quickly typed a "k" back to Rachel and turned to Dee with what I hoped was a normal smile, but the pounding in my head chose that moment to hit me with a fresh wave of pain. "Are you alright?" she asked, concern marring the perfection of her elfin features.

I shook my head. "Another rough day." At the tilt of her head, I continued. "Junior year might be the death of me." I smiled again and chuckled a little as I slipped my phone into my bag. When I glanced back at Dee, she was staring at the pocket where I'd put my phone. She smiled, her blue eyes twinkling.

"I know what you mean. I can't wait for high school to be over. I'm so ready to move on." She uncapped her pen and flipped open her spiral notebook.

"Oh, I don't think you'll need that. We're taking a practice test today *if* Ms. Jordan ever gets here." I twisted my neck right then left, trying to alleviate some of the tension and lessen the headache.

Dee watched me. "Teachers never seem to be where you want them, and when they are, they only see what they want to see."

I turned to her, but she'd turned to the front just as Ms. Jordan came in with a handful of papers.

"Sorry I'm late. I had a disagreement with the copy machine." She smiled and held the papers above her head triumphantly. "But never fear. I have the practice test." A general groan issued from around the room. Even though we were all here voluntarily, no one likes the "t" word, practice or not. She started counting out papers and handing them to the person in the front of each row to pass back. "I've included an answer sheet at the back for you to write the letter of your choice instead of bubbling in the answers. This will make it easier for me to grade. Complete as many questions as you can in the hour we have, and we'll use these over the next couple of sessions to get into some strategies for test taking."

I leaned down to grab a pen from my bag just as the test landed on the desk. I signed my name to the front and looked at Dee. She was recapping her pen and gathering her notebook. I raised my brows as she stood.

"I just got a message from my grandfather. He needs me to come home. I'll see you soon." She turned and left before I could say anything.

I sighed as I looked at the test in front of me. I tore the answer sheet from the back and tried to focus on the questions. It was as bad as I had thought it would be, and when Ms. Jordan called time, I had five unanswered questions. I waited in my seat as the other students walked to her desk to hand in their papers. When only two students remained, I gathered my pages to re-staple the answer sheet to the questions. I thought I'd do Ms. Jordan a favor and take Dee's paper up with me, so Ms. Jordan wouldn't have to walk back to get it. But when I turned to grab the sheets, there weren't any on her desk. Shrugging, I figured someone else must have done it, and I walked to the front as the last of the kids passed me on their way out.

"Thanks for staying," Ms. Jordan said with a smile. "I know you weren't feeling well, and I want you to keep that in mind when you get your results back next week. Don't be too hard on yourself." She winked.

"You know me well, Ms. Jordan." She knew I'd beat myself up over my poor results.

"It's one practice on one day that you were sick. So no worries, okay? It's not the real thing, and I'll bet when you see your answers next week, you'll kick yourself over the answers you would have chosen had you felt better."

I took her stapler and reattached the page. As I handed it to her, she said, "You're not superhuman, girl. Take a day off if you're sick."

I nodded. "Yes, ma'am, thanks." I went back to my seat and lifted my bag just as my phone buzzed. Rachel had messaged again, telling me to meet them out front. When I dropped it back into my bag, Dee flashed into my mind. She hadn't had a bag, no purse, no backpack, nothing but her notebook and pen. That skirt couldn't have had pockets, not the way it was made. She left when she said she'd gotten a message from her grandfather, but I hadn't seen a phone.

I looked back at Ms. Jordan who was putting the papers in her bag. I was going to ask her if she knew Dee, but her phone rang. She picked it up and swiped the screen.

"Hey, Mark," she said with the kind of grin girls only get when a guy they like talks to them. She covered the bottom of her phone with her fingers and met my eyes. "Did you need something, Ria?"

I shook my head. "No, see you tomorrow." I wasn't going to interrupt a call with her boyfriend when I could just ask tomorrow. I turned back to Dee's desk. Something wasn't right. And I was beginning to wonder if it was me.

CHAPTER 16

"So now that we aren't at school, I gotta know what happened to you today?" Rachel had spread her history book and notebook across my bed, but she wasn't working on the terms. She was lying on her back, scrolling on the phone in front of her face. I, on the other hand, was flipping pages in my history book searching for the next definition on the list.

"You could help, you know. We need to get these done if you want to go to that football game," I said, trying to deflect her question. I usually shared everything with Rachel. She was my only friend, but the last few days had been too much. I didn't know if was ready to have my BFF look at me like I was nuts. Rachel loved me, but I couldn't predict how she'd take my crazy waking-dream episode in Coach Joseph's room. Normal teenagers didn't see their teacher's face and have some kind of paranormal episode.

"Oh, take a break. We've been working for over an hour, and we only have four left. What does finishing this have to do with the game anyway?" She dropped her phone beside her and rolled to face me, her left arm propping up her head.

I tossed my pen into the center of my book and leaned back against the pillows, letting my eyes fall shut. My headache was better, and I probably could have fallen asleep right there if not for Rachel's penetrating stare. She wasn't going to let it go.

Sighing, I lifted myself from my pillows. "I just thought if we take some pressure off we could have a better time Friday night."

She pursed her lips and narrowed her amber eyes. "Spill it. What's going on with you?"

We stayed like that, a cowboy stare-down, for at least thirty seconds till I broke. I rolled my eyes and groaned. "I'm not sleeping. I had …a …nightmare, and it's really, I don't know, weighing on me for some reason."

She sat up and crossed her legs in front of her. "What kind of nightmare? Tell me about it."

I looked away toward my mirror. I saw myself as she saw me then, hair mussed, circles under my eyes, and the tension from the past day slumping my shoulders like a beaten animal. I told her about the dream, the girl, the room, the boy in the door. She listened without interruption. "And when we walked into Coach's room today, well, he said the same thing as the dream boy, and I guess my brain just overloaded." I lifted my hands and dropped them into my lap. "I think it was a panic attack." I wasn't sure I wanted to share what happened when I went back into the room. I wanted to see what her reaction to the dream was before I told her anything else.

Rachel gave me a small smile and crawled over the books and notebooks separating us until she was cozied up next to me. She put her arm around me and squeezed. I put my forehead against the side of her head, and she wrapped her other arm across the front of my shoulders. She squeezed again and kept her arms around me while she said, "You have been my best friend since you moved here. I really think God brought your family here because I needed someone. I know how crazy that sounds, but like I've told you before, I didn't have any real friends till you, and I know you, Ria Gabriel. You have been driving yourself too hard since August. You don't have to be perfect, and you have to stop pushing to be. You need a day off."

I pulled her arm down and held her hand, but she kept her other arm wrapped around me. Our eyes met again, and I lifted one corner of my mouth and nodded. "Yeah, Mom said the same thing. But you know how hard it is to catch up when you miss."

She nodded. "You're just under a lot of stress. You need a good night's sleep." She closed both of our books and notebooks.

"What are you doing? We're almost done," I said, shaking my head.

"No, we are done. I'll do the last four, type the whole list, and send it to your email." She raised her hand before I could say anything. "I'm doing it tonight, at home, and you'll have it when you wake up, so don't worry." She packed her bag and hefted it onto her shoulder.

"But I thought you were going to stay for dinner." Rachel hadn't come over just to do history terms. She was hoping to spend time with Jake, too, even though she hadn't said it.

"Hey, you're my friend, and you come first always." She grinned mischievously. "Besides, I figure I could use a few goodwill points in Heaven. I've been having some impure thoughts lately, and—"

I plugged my fingers into my ears. "Gross! Stop!"

Rachel giggled. "I'm gonna say bye to Jake and your parents, then I'll head out." She pointed at me, one hand on the doorknob. "You go to bed."

"I love you, friend," I said.

"Love you, too," she said over her shoulder as she walked out.

I tossed my books from my bed and walked to my bathroom. I had some nighttime cough medicine in my bathroom that Mom bought last winter when I had the flu. A couple teaspoons of that, and I knew I'd be out. I poured the sticky red liquid into the dosage cup and swallowed it, then filled the cup again with water to rinse my mouth. A soft knock came from the door.

"Come in," I called. Mom walked in, a dish towel in her hand and concern wrinkling her brow.

"Rachel said you were going to bed. You okay?" We met halfway across my bedroom, and she pulled my forehead to her lips--not for a kiss, so much as to see if I had fever.

"I've had a headache all day, and I just want to go to bed." The day rested on my sagging shoulders, and she rubbed my upper arm.

"Okay. I'll save some chicken for you in case you nap awhile and decide you're hungry." She turned off my lamp on the way out of my room, leaving the room bathed in moonlight and the light from my bathroom night light. "Goodnight, honey."

The door clicked shut behind her, and I pulled off my clothes. I thought I'd left my nightgown on the end of the bed this morning, like I usually do, but it wasn't there. Maybe Rachel had knocked it off when she got on the bed earlier. I knelt and searched under the bed but no luck. I was about to turn the lamp back on when I saw it hanging over the top of the full-length. I was certain it hadn't been there earlier when I'd seen my reflection as Rachel and I sat on the bed. I walked to the mirror, the hair on my neck tingling as a chill passed over me. I could see behind me in the mirror, but I felt like I wasn't alone. I didn't want to turn around. I didn't want to know, but I had to. I turned my head slowly, but my body refused to follow. Nothing. There was nothing behind me.

"Ria."

I whipped my head around so quickly I stumbled and had to grab for the mirror frame to keep from falling. My face was inches from the mirror. Blue eyes, the same blue eyes as I'd seen before, glowed back at me. The pendant flashed in the light from the bathroom. I squeezed my eyes closed and fell to the floor.

****

"Miriam, are you going to school today?" I opened my eyes, and Mom was standing over me, pushing the hair off my forehead. I sat up in a rush that made my head spin. I was in my purple gown tucked between sheets that looked like I hadn't moved all night. My mind raced as I looked toward the mirror. I'd seen her eyes again last night, right? I'd been reaching for my gown and then …then what? The last thing I remembered was that pair of blue eyes staring back from my face.

"Honey, are you okay?" Mom pressed her hand to my forehead.

I pushed it away. "I'm fine. I took some cold medicine last night to help me sleep better, and I think I'm a little groggy." That had to be it. I hadn't eaten much all day, and the medicine must have hit me harder than I'd thought. I'd imagined the whole thing or dreamed it before the medicine really kicked in. I couldn't remember any other dreams, and from the tidy condition of the bed, I must have slept soundly.

"Did it work? You have a better night?" Mom went into my bathroom to collect dirty towels. She threw them in a basket she must have brought in with her.

I nodded. "Yeah, headache's gone." Which was true—mostly. The ache was still there in the tension in my neck and shoulders, but I needed a normal day, a regular day with no dream boys or freaky blue eyes. I needed a typical day at school, my safe place. If I told her I still didn't feel like myself, she'd make me stay home, and I needed to face the day, not hide from it. I was afraid if I hid, I'd never get out of bed again. I needed to be myself today, not the me I'd been for the last few days, and to do that I needed school.

I tugged at the pendant still hanging around my neck. All of this madness had started when I got the necklace. It seemed connected in some way, which sounded completely crazy. I thought again of Mom's offer to take me to the jewelry store to have it removed, but that felt wrong, like I was actually giving in to this insane idea that a necklace was creating nightmares and headaches.

I looked in the mirror again. It was just a necklace. It had to be, and if it wasn't, I wouldn't let it win. Removing it would mean admitting I believed what was happening was supernatural, or it'd be like declaring I'd been beaten by a dumb piece of jewelry—no, by something connected to a dumb piece of jewelry, something I couldn't see or touch, something I was letting get to me, invade my head. I didn't want to take it off until I was in control again. If I took it off now, it felt like a defeat in some way. It wouldn't win. I would.

Throwing back the cover, I swung my legs over the side of the bed. "I'm going to school."

CHAPTER 17

"I'm so excited! I haven't been to a game in forever!"

I rolled my eyes without fear of hurting Rachel's feelings. She was too consumed with outlining her lips and applying the perfect amount of gloss. If she'd squealed in delight once, she'd done it ten times in the past hour. Jake had to be at the stadium early with the rest of the team, so Rachel and I had gotten a ride with Mom and Dad but planned on riding home with Jake after the game.

After two days without weird dreams, I was feeling like myself. I'd taken more cough medicine Thursday night, and just like before, I'd slept dreamlessly and hard. I'd apologized to Coach Joseph for acting so strangely and had given him the same excuse Rachel had supplied the night we were working on those definitions. Stress made people act crazy, and that was exactly what had happened to me. It was like sleep had reset my system, and I hadn't heard voices or seen creepy blue eyes again.

I looked at my reflection in the mirror of the girls' restroom. I'd even managed a little makeup tonight and had put on my favorite jeans and school sweatshirt to support the team.

Rachel's smile was wide when she turned to me. "See any on my teeth?" I shook my head, and she glanced back at herself before grabbing my arm with a grip that was just short of painful. "Come on. I don't want to miss any of Jake's playing."

I laughed as we walked out into the stadium lobby, which was mostly empty. Bethel was one of our biggest rivals, and most of the crowd was steering clear of the concession stand for the same reason Rachel was in a hurry. It was close, with Thomasville winning by only two points in the middle of the third quarter. Besides the two of us, only a handful of people were at the concession stand, where band parents were dishing out nachos and hot dogs.

"Hey, I'm gonna grab a soda before we go back. You want one?" Rachel asked, digging in her designer crossbody bag for some cash.

"No, I'm good." While Rachel got in line, I looked at the trophy case across from the concession stand window. Years of tradition stared back from the photos of previous teams that dated all the way back to the 30s. I smiled at the crazy striped uniforms and leather helmets and wondered how Mom and Dad would feel about Jake playing in so little protection. Rachel was still waiting, so I wandered down the hall that ran beside the concession stand.

Lining the hall were the framed photos of graduating classes dating back to the school's founding hung three frames tall on the cement wall. As I walked past the rows of faces, the severe middle parts and sleek bobs morphed into oil-laden pompadours and beehive updos I would never have had the patience or desire to create. As the glam of the 50s and 60s gave way to the unkempt mustaches and winged flips of the 70s, my phone rang. It was Rachel.

I slid the green phone icon and said, "I'm in the class hall."

"Where?" she asked.

"The hall with all the class photos."

"Well, come on." I could hear the impatience in her voice as she rattled the phone, probably putting away the change from her soda purchase.

"Alright, I'll be there in a second." But when I turned, a photo of a young man drew my attention. I couldn't explain it, but it seemed to jump out at me, demanding closer inspection. "Hey, why don't you go on back to the stands? I'll catch up in a minute. I think I'll get something from the concession stand after all," I added. I didn't want Rachel to know I was hanging back to study a photo of some random guy. I was back to being me again, and it would sound completely mental to admit I wanted a closer look at a stranger's photo.

"Okay, see you in a second."

I pushed the red phone icon on my screen and moved toward the frame, which was the bottom frame in the grouping of three in front of me. "Class of 86" was written in swirling font at the top. At first glance, there was nothing out of the ordinary about the boy who was on the second row of faces. He had dark brown hair and smooth tan skin. His sweater was light-blue with a tiny red man riding a horse on the upper-left of his chest. He had a handsome face with features that probably made him popular with the girls in the class of 86. I stared into his eyes, and realization slapped me in the face.

His eyes were so vividly blue that piercing would have been the most accurate word to describe them. They were lined by inky, thick lashes and were so alive I expected him to blink at any second. The hand-written calligraphy beneath his name read "Philip Ezra." I lifted my phone and slid my finger over the camera icon, zooming in on Philip's photo. If I'd thought about it too hard, I would never have taken a pic of his photo. I knew it wasn't logical, but I couldn't stop myself. I needed this photo. I touched the screen and captured his face in my phone.

Looking into his eyes seemed so …familiar. I shivered. I knew those eyes. I'd seen them in my room. Then the voice invaded my head again. "Free me, Ria."

CHAPTER 18

He couldn't be connected to the girl in my dreams. It made no sense, but none of this had made sense since it all began. I stared at his mesmerizing eyes. How was any of this possible?

I was staring at the phone so hard I didn't realize I'd walked back into the lobby until I almost collided with a girl coming out of the restroom. When I looked up to apologize, I saw Dee's face.

"Hey, Ria!" Dee smiled.

"Dee! Sorry I nearly ran over you." I tucked my phone into my back pocket.

Her eyes twinkled. "You were pretty absorbed. Could it be a message from a boy?"

"No, definitely not," I said with a chuckle.

She narrowed her eyes. "You sure about that?"

I had this eerie feeling as she tilted her head and scanned me from head to toe. Could she have seen Philip's photo before I put my phone away?

"Why aren't you out there enjoying the game?" she asked. "Your brother plays, doesn't he?"

I nodded. "He's the quarterback. I was about to head back to the stands. Wanna sit with me and my friend Rachel?" I motioned toward the doors that led to the stands. The two moms standing behind the concession stand window leaned close together and whispered as their eyes cut in our direction. I didn't recognize either woman. Did they know Dee?

She scrunched up her nose and shook her head. "I was actually about to leave." She glanced around and crossed her arms over her off-white peasant blouse. The flared sleeves fell back, revealing a gold charm bracelet and that beautiful gold watch she'd worn the first time I'd seen her. She shrugged. "Not really my thing. I thought I'd give it a try, but not as much fun as I hoped."

"Aw, come on—" I started to reach for her hand but remembered she was a germaphobe and pulled back "—I'd like for you to meet my friend."

Her face lit. "I have a better idea! Why don't you come with me? I was planning on getting some coffee at a little place I know. You could come along."

"That sounds fun. I'm not really all about the game, but I don't think Rachel would want to go. She has a date with my brother after the game."

Dee's mouth pulled to one side. "That's a little awkward, tagging along with Rachel and Jake on their date."

I nodded. "I know, right?" Then it hit me. She'd called Jake by name. "Do you know Jake?"

She blinked in confusion. "Everyone knows the quarterback." She smiled. "Come on, you know you want to go. Who wants to tag along with their brother on a date? You'll be the third wheel."

Her smile was beguiling, and she was completely right. I hadn't really wanted to go, and here was my chance to get out of it and not just go home like the loser I usually felt like on weekend nights. "Alright, let's go tell Rachel."

Her smile wilted a little. "Why don't I just wait here for you? I'd rather not fight the crowd again." She motioned with her chin toward the group of grownups who always hung out along the fence that ran beside the field. The mostly male crowd made it a challenge to get from the lobby to the seats, and it always felt like *I* had just been thrown into the game when I managed to escape.

"Maybe you're right. I could just message her." I pulled my phone from my back pocket.

She stepped toward the door that led to the parking lot. "Let's do it out here." She flipped her fingers toward the concession stand. "I feel like we have an audience."

I glanced over my shoulder at the women who still stood staring at us from the concession window. I lowered my voice and leaned closer to Dee. "I noticed. What's their deal?"

Dee shrugged. "Jealous of our youth no doubt." She chuckled. "Let's go outside."

I nodded and walked ahead of her, holding the door as she walked out. I sent Rachel a text telling her I was going to head out. Rachel's face immediately popped up on my screen, and my phone buzzed as it rang.

Before I could even say hello, she said, "You're leaving? Why?"

"I met up with Dee in the lobby, remember the girl I met at ACT study group? We're going to get some coffee, let you and Jake have a date night without me."

"Ria," Rachel whined like a five-year-old. "I wanted you to come along with us. It's our first real date."

"Important word there is 'date,' Rach. You don't need me along. It'll be weird and, well, gross. I know how long you've wanted a date with Jake, and—" Dee was mouthing "third wheel" as she watched me talk with Rachel "—I'll just be a third wheel." Dee smiled broadly and checked her watch as though we were on a schedule.

Rachel sighed. "But you'll miss the rest of the game. Can't you and Dee come watch and then go? It'll give me a chance to meet her."

Dee was shaking her head. I guess my phone volume was louder than I thought, and she could hear Rachel over the speaker. "By the time we fight the crowd, it'll be over. You can call me later and tell me all about it." Then I considered what that might be and amended my statement. "Well, maybe not *all* about it. Love you, friend," I singsonged into the phone in hopes of softening the fact that I was leaving her alone in the stands.

"Yeah, yeah, you're ditching me." I could practically hear her pouting.

I did feel a little guilty about leaving Rachel, but she's the one who made it all awkward by going on a date with my brother. Then again, I was the one who encouraged it.

"Don't be mad. I'll talk to you later." I disconnected the call before she could drag me into more guilt.

Dee winked and waved her hand. "Come on before we're too late."

"I hope you have a car because I just blew off my ride." I smiled, but Dee walked ahead and glanced back over her shoulder.

"It's not far. Don't worry. I'll keep you safe and sound." One corner of her mouth turned up, and her blue eyes held mine until she turned back around. For the second time tonight, a shiver sprinted along my spine.

CHAPTER 19

I'd never noticed the coffee shop snuggled between two larger buildings about a block from the school, but I'd never really walked around the area much since I usually rode to school with Jake or had Mom drop me off. The plate glass window sported a white neon cup and saucer with a swirl of blue neon smoke emerging from its rim. The unpainted brick walls, wooden booths, and low-hanging single bulbs covered with tortoise shell globes lent an air of secrecy to the place. I could easily imagine clandestine meetings between lovers or spies.

We took a booth near the back though only one other person was in the shop. A white haired old woman sat across the room with her back to me, but she appeared to be reading a novel while she sipped from a mug that had to hold at least four cups.

"I need to use the little girls' room. Order me a coffee, okay?" Dee slid from the booth before the barista made her way over. I nodded and pulled the menu from where it leaned between the wall and a sugar dispenser. A catalogue of beverages with complicated titles like half-soy quad macchiato had me thinking that Dee had the right idea in just wanting coffee.

The barista's smile had probably been much cheerier at the beginning of her shift. "What can I get you?" She pulled a pencil from her messy blonde bun and a small notepad from her front pocket.

"Two coffees and some creamer please." I laid my phone on the table and slid my finger over the sensor to unlock it, checking for messages.

"You want a double?" she asked.

"A double?" I glanced up from my phone.

"Like a large cup that holds two coffees." She looked at the empty seat across from me.

I realized she must have missed Dee when we came in. "No, my friend is in the restroom."

She glanced toward the door that led to the ladies' room and nodded slowly. "Oh, okay, two coffees with creamer on the side. Be right back."

Dee returned right after the barista set the cups down and went back behind the counter to wash equipment and do whatever she needed for closing.

"This is a great place," I said, eying the sweets and sandwich display case. "I bet they serve a good lunch." I poured cream and sugar into my cup and stirred as Dee nodded.

"I haven't been here in a while, but they used to. I liked to come here to read and escape."

"Escape?" I pushed the sugar toward her, but she shook her head and crossed her arms atop the table.

"You know, from whatever." She shook her head and absently ran her finger in circles around the front of her watch, looking down as though she could see more on the table than the scarred surface. "Family, school—whatever."

I studied the soft fringe of dark lashes along her high cheekbones. With her tiny nose and Cupid 's bow lips, she didn't look like a girl who never had any problems. She looked like the kind of girl whose life fell in place as perfectly as standing dominoes. But as I watched her finger twirl in faster circles, I realized how wrong my illusion must have been. She met my eyes as though she knew what I was thinking.

"Things aren't ever easy as they seem." She leaned back against the booth, dropping her hands in her lap.

I sipped my coffee as she continued to watch me. Her stare made me uneasy. "So, I asked my brother if he knew you, but he said he didn't."

One corner of her mouth turned up. "Not surprising. I've seen him, who hasn't? The best looking quarterback Thomasville has ever had, but I wouldn't expect him to have seen me."

I laughed. "Are you kidding me? As pretty as you are, I was shocked when he said he didn't know you. He's a bit of a—"

"Man whore? Yeah, I've noticed that, too." She crossed her arms on the table again. "And now he's dating your friend. That's not awkward." She rolled her eyes and raised her hand dramatically before grinning.

"Tell me about it." I picked up my cup and captured it's warmth in my hands.

"What happens when he breaks her heart? Will she blame you?"

I shrugged and slowly shook my head. What would happen? I couldn't believe Rachel would blame me, but I had no way of knowing for sure. We'd been as close as sisters, but would that friendship withstand the anger of a break up? As much as I hoped for the best for Rachel, I didn't have as much faith in Jake. Again, I wished I'd never pushed the two of them together.

"You just never know what people will do, how they'll react, until you put their backs to the wall. Hope she doesn't exchange your friendship for your brother's attention." Dee checked her watch. "Oh, wow, I didn't realize how late it was. I've got to run."

I glanced at my phone. It was only 9:45. "You're leaving?"

She nodded and stood. "I have to get home." She looked at the table and smiled almost sadly. "Thanks for coming with me. I haven't been out in forever. We'll have to do it again sometime." Then she turned and walked to the door without looking back.

She left. She just left. I shook my head and blinked, still not believing Dee had left me sitting here. I walked to the counter as the barista came through a swinging door that separated a small kitchen from the front. She touched the screen of the register's computer and said, "That'll be $5.72."

I reached into my pocket and pulled out a ten. I glanced to my right at the old woman who was still sitting in the booth. The bulb above her made her white hair nearly glow. Manicured red nails held her novel open, and when she shifted her left hand to grab her mug, light reflected off a large ring.

I hardly noticed as the barista handed me the change. Light flashed from the ring again as the woman brought the mug to her mouth, and I finally looked closely at her face. Her skin wrinkled softly around her eyes behind silver half-moon glasses, and her red lipstick held firm as though it didn't dare fade even against the onslaught of the coffee mug. My mind flashed to a red shirt and heavy silver bracelets as my hand automatically found the pendant.

I nodded to the barista as she thanked me and walked toward the woman. She was so absorbed in her book that she didn't notice me until I was right beside her. When she finally glanced up over her glasses, I expected those penetrating blue eyes that had stared so forcefully into mine at the estate sale where I'd been given the necklace, and though her eyes were blue, they were missing that intensity. I looked down at the ring that had first drawn my eye. A sapphire the color of twilight surrounded by diamonds sparkled in the light. It had to be her.

Her white brows drew together, but she smiled. "Did you need something, dear?"

"You don't remember me?" I sat in the booth across from her though I hadn't been invited. I needed an explanation from the mysterious woman who'd given me a valuable antique and then promptly vanished.

She removed her glasses and tilted her head. "Hmm, you don't look old enough to have been one of my students. Are you Sarah's granddaughter?"

I shook my head. "No, ma'am. We met a few weeks ago at an estate sale."

"We met at the estate sale? Are you certain?" Her brow wrinkled even more as studied me.

I pointed to the sapphire. "You asked me to help you pick out that ring, but you said it was for your granddaughter."

She held up her hand as though only just noticing the ring. "I remember the sale and, of course, buying the ring, but I don't have a granddaughter, dear. Maybe you have me confused with someone else."

Impossible, not with the ring as proof, but I didn't want to be rude and say that to her. "You don't remember buying me this?" I stood and stretched across the table, holding the pendant out so she could get a closer look.

She touched the pendant, then put her glasses back on to inspect it further. After she dropped her hand, she shook her head. "I'm afraid not, but it's beautiful, quality, too. You say I bought it for you?"

I nodded and sat again, but she only laughed. "Well, either I'm getting more absent-minded than I thought, or you have the wrong person. You said we spoke at the estate sale?" She shook her head with a chuckle. "Here I thought thirty-five years with teenagers would have made me crazy when actually it's retirement. You know the other day I couldn't find my glasses. I must have searched for an hour before I finally realized they were on top of my head. I would think I would remember buying that necklace, but…" She shook her head and chuckled.

I attempted to smile past my disappointment and confusion. How could she possibly not remember me? "I'm sorry I disturbed y——" I started to stand, but she waved her hand toward the seat.

"Stay awhile. It's been so long since I've gotten to talk to a young person—well, that I can recall anyway." She smiled again. "I thought when I left teaching that I'd be content if I never had to mess with another teenager as long as I lived, but—" she shrugged "—let's just say it took leaving to make me realize why I was really teaching in the first place. Do you go to school at Thomasville?"

I nodded. "Yes, ma'am. I'm a junior there. My name's Ria." I extended my hand across the space, and when she eagerly clasped it, I remembered the papery feel of her skin that Saturday when we first met.

"I'm Ruth Claudia, former teacher and now—what is it you kids say? A slacker." She sipped her coffee, and a drop slipped from the mug's lip, landing on the table near her hands. I passed a napkin from the dispenser on the table near me. "Oh, thank you, dear."

My smile was genuine this time. "So you don't have any grandchildren?"

"Oh no! I do." She pulled her phone from the massive purse beside her and scrolled through her photos till she came to one of two smiling boys with blond hair. "Joel and Jesse, fraternal twins who just turned fifteen." Her mouth turned down. "They live about seven hours away, so I only see them on Christmas break and occasionally in the summer."

I handed her phone back, and she slipped it back into her cavernous bag. Her face lit again. "And they don't wear jewelry, so I must have been wishful thinking the day we met."

"Did you teach here in Thomasville?" I asked.

She took a sip of her coffee and nodded. "I did. I taught English and history for a bit. I thought I couldn't wait to be retired." She reached across and patted my hand where it lay on the table. "Don't hurry your life away, dear. It'll go faster than you dreamed possible."

My phone buzzed, and I saw a message from Mom telling me she'd run into Rachel after the game and asking if I was okay. I realized then that I would need a ride since I'd decided not to go with Rachel and Jake. I messaged her back to wait for me at the car.

"It was nice meeting you, Ms. Claudia," I said, standing and sliding my phone into my back pocket. "I've got to go meet my mom."

"It was my pleasure, Ria. I'm here often. Maybe we'll run into each other again." She picked up her novel, and I left to walk back to campus. How could this mystery get any stranger? A necklace I didn't want bought by a woman who couldn't remember buying it for me. This enigma was becoming a part of me. I would figure this out or die trying—and that scared me more than any dream.

CHAPTER 20

"I know you're upset, but I promise I'll get to the bottom of it on Monday."

He's so kind, but he just doesn't understand. How could he? He's one of them. He's always taking their side. I cry against my pillow trying to smother the sobs, so he thinks I'm okay as I nod. He's my brother, and it's not him I ache to hurt.

"Now, sit up. I have something for you." He wiggles his hand into the pocket of his khakis and pulls out a red satin bag about the size of his palm. The bed squeaks a little as I sit up and tug at my nightgown. My stained dress lies in a ruined pink puddle next to my bed. I haven't shown Mother. She'll want an explanation, and I haven't thought of anything yet. If she finds out what happened at school, she'll be mad again and accuse me of not trying harder to be like him. I squash the moment of anger I feel at him and remind myself again it's not his fault.

I wipe my nose with my palm, and he smiles the way he does when they're around, the smile that makes all those girls call our house. His eyes, my eyes too, look so different in his face. I look freakish, like a nocturnal animal with too-big eyes; he is handsome and confident.

I take the red bag and pull open the black satin drawstring. The chain is silver, and the pendant's stone captures the light and reflects it in a fiery burst of colors. I close it in my palm and spring toward him, wrapping my arms around his neck.

He chuckles. "I know it's not gold, and you really like gold, but I saw it in the antique store window and thought it might bring you some luck."

"I don't care. I love it!" I turn my back and hand him the

necklace. As he drapes it around my neck, I say, "I'll never take it off. Thank you, Philip."

****

I opened my eyes slowly without the terror of the last dream and touched the pendant where it lay against my chest. It was the same as the pendant in the dream. Taking my phone from my bedside table, I searched for and found the picture I'd taken of Philip Ezra. He was the boy I'd just seen sitting on a bed that wasn't mine, hugging me, comforting me.

My rational mind insisted that it was only a dream caused by the photo, but my heart said it wasn't. As horrible as the last dream had been, this one left me feeling safe, happy even.

Was it possible that Philip Ezra had given this necklace to his sister? That his sister was the girl who was hiding in the dark, afraid of the bullies taunting her? I touched the pendant, and a feeling like towels fresh from the dryer passed through me. For the first time, the necklace didn't leave me unsettled. It left me comforted. A loving brother had given the pendant to his sister with the promise of taking care of her. He'd picked it out because he thought she would like it, out of genuine love for her. I thought of Jake and the bracelet he'd made for me tucked away in my jewelry box.

Could I actually be touching the same necklace that a loving brother had given to his tortured sister? I glanced across the room into the darkened mirror where the moonlight leant a glow to the silver clover. I needed to find out more about Phillip but more importantly, I needed to find out more about his sister.

CHAPTER 21

Rachel bounced on my bed bright and early Saturday morning, despite my efforts to push her off. She laughed as I put the pillow over my head to block her out.

"Get up! I didn't believe it when your mom told me you were still sleeping!" Rachel put her arms on either side of my body and rocked me back and forth with a strength that surprised me. Her jostling guaranteed that I wasn't going to get to go back to sleep. She jerked the pillow away and tossed it on the floor.

"Why are you here so early?" I pushed her back so I could sit up.

She feigned indignation, fluttering her lashes and putting her hand to her chest. "Rude!" Then she smiled. "Jake invited me over."

"At the crack of dawn?" I grumped, swinging my legs over the bedside and walking to the bathroom. I didn't bother to close the door as I did my morning business.

Rachel sat on the bed, squeezing the pillow she hadn't tossed. "It's not the crack of dawn. It's past 9:00. He wants to spend the whole day together. Isn't that the sweetest thing?" She didn't let me respond but went on gushing. "Oh, Ria! We had such a good time after the game. Nearly the whole team went out to Bethany's for burgers since that's Jake's favorite, and he threw that amazing pass to win. Then we went for ice cream, just the two of us, and held hands, and—"

I stepped out of the bathroom, toothbrush sticking out of mouth, and held up my hands. "Enough," I slobbered around my brush.

She grinned wickedly and fell back on my bed. "I'm so happy."

I went to the bathroom and finished, then grabbed a sweatshirt to slip over my cami, leaving my pajama bottoms on since I didn't have any plans. I pulled my hair in a ponytail and looked down at her glowing face.

"Hey, where'd you go last night anyway?" she asked, sitting again and relinquishing my pillow. "You didn't return my messages."

I shooed her off the bed and straightened the covers. "A coffee shop near the school. I was tired when I got home, and I went to bed." I picked up the pillows and threw them on the bed.

"Tired? It was only like 10:00 or something when I texted." She picked up my phone and unlocked it with my code. It never bothered me before that Rachel knew my code, but her blatant disregard for my privacy irritated me this morning. I jerked the phone from her hands.

"It's bad enough you woke me up on my one day to sleep in; you don't have to go through my phone, too, *Mom*."

This time, Rachel's affront was real. She looked at me with hurt. "Geez, sorry!" She held up her hands in surrender. "What's wrong with you? You ditched *me* last night, remember?"

"Oh 'cause what I really want to do is see my best friend drool all over my brother." I rolled my eyes.

Rachel's mouth fell open, and her eyes rounded. She gasped. "You supported this relationship!"

In an instant, I was completely angry, consumed with it. Rachel had nothing on her mind but Jake lately. She didn't have time to talk to me about my problems. She'd only wanted me to go with her last night because she was worried about keeping Jake's attention. Dee had been right. Rachel was more concerned about Jake than me. "Relationship? Rachel, you don't have a relationship. Jake has never dated a girl longer than a few weeks, and then what? It'll be completely weird and awkward. I wish I'd never asked Jake to take you out."

Rachel's eyes filled with tears, and for a second, I was sorry for the harsh words, but the rage came rushing back quickly. A voice in my head said, "She's just like the others. She only cares about herself without bothering to think how you feel."

And then I opened my door and said, "You only came over because of Jake. I suggest you go wake him."

Rachel's jaw dropped even closer to her chest before she snapped it shut and stood. A tear ran down her face, and she brushed it away brusquely as her mouth tightened. She passed without looking at me.

CHAPTER 22

I spent the morning in my room until I heard Jake and Rachel leave around noon. Mom came in shortly after Jake's truck pulled out of the driveway. She didn't knock, telling me she meant serious business.

"Alright, what happened? Rachel came downstairs crying her eyes out." She put her hands on her hips. "And your brother was so mad he was ready to come up here and drag you out."

I tossed *Jane Eyre* to the floor. I'd read the same page three times, so clearly I wasn't concentrating anyway. I'd heard Rachel crying when she and Jake walked past my room. She had gone to his room after I'd thrown her out. Now that I'd calmed down, I could see how irrational I'd been, and normally I would've apologized for acting like a total jerk, but I just couldn't seem to force my feet to go downstairs. Every time I'd walked to the door, I'd stopped with my hand on the knob and turned back. What I said was mean, but it was still sort of true. "All she wants to talk about is Jake."

"Is that what you said?" She scooted my feet over and sat facing me on the bed.

I shrugged and glanced down at the comforter. "Sort of."

I didn't have to see Mom's face to know she was giving me the disappointed look. "Uh huh," she hummed. Moms have that inner bullcrap meter, and I'm guessing Rebekah Gabriel's was buzzing uncontrollably. "You hurt her. You need to apologize."

Crossing my arms, I met her eyes. But when she tilted her head and raised one pale brow, my attempt at a stare down ended, and I sighed. "Yeah, probably, but—"

She held up one finger. "No, Miriam, she's your friend. She's dating your brother, and you love her. Whatever is going on with you needs to stop. You're moody and distant, and you know I'm right."

I nodded and dropped my head again, feeling an awful lot like I did when I was six and broke Mom's favorite vase, then blamed it on Jake.

"Your father and I will be leaving in about half an hour. Can I trust you not to fight with Jake while we're gone?"

Mom and Dad told me last night that they were going out of town for the night to an estate sale that Dad had seen online. They had booked a hotel room close to the sale venue, so they could be there as soon as the door opened. I nodded again. "Yes, ma'am." I felt stupid and childish, which I assume was Mom's purpose in taking me to task for my harsh words.

"And when they come home later, you will apologize to them both."

"Yes, ma'am," I mumbled again.

Mom stood, then leaned down to kiss my forehead. "I love you, honey, but you can't control their feelings." She smiled. "Lock the door behind us, and don't forget to bring in Cain if Jake isn't back by dark."

"Love you, too." When she opened the door to leave, I said, "Thanks, Mom."

****

I saved my AP history paper on Mary Todd Lincoln and closed my laptop before leaning back and rubbing my forehead. Picking up my phone, I glanced at the time, 10:22, well past dark. Jake hadn't texted, but that was expected. I hadn't bothered to text either him or Rachel. I'd told Mom I'd apologize when they came home, and technically they weren't home yet. I was going to use the loophole as my excuse. She was right. I needed to apologize, but that wouldn't make it any easier to swallow my pride and admit I was a jerk.

I sighed loudly, dreading the chore of bringing Cain inside. Cain and I had a relationship based solely on ignoring each other. After our last encounter when I thought he'd take my head off, I'd avoided him as much as possible. I doubted a whole bag of treats would coax him inside, but I had to try. And honestly, as much as I hated the hassle of bringing him in, my practical side wouldn't let me forget I did feel safer with him here and Mom and Dad gone.

I slid on my slippers and trudged downstairs to the kitchen, not bothering to flip on any lights. Mom always kept a small lamp on the counter which she'd rigged to a timer and set to come on before dark. Along the tops of the cabinets among the antique bottles and canisters, Mom had strung white Christmas lights that came on at night also, so I knew there'd be enough light to bring Cain inside. The lights reflected in the huge mirror hanging above the breakfast table.

I unlocked the French doors and stepped out onto the patio, rubbing my arms against the chill air. I tucked the hair that had slipped from my ponytail behind my ear as Cain trotted up, the tags on his collar ring jingling.

"Come on." But Cain plopped down on his haunches. "No, up, inside," I commanded. Cain tilted his head, the light from the patio reflecting in his chocolate-brown eyes. He shook his head as though he were answering and laid down on his front paws. I sighed again. "You aren't going to make this easy, are you?" I shifted toward him, and he jerked to a half-crouch, the way he did when he played keep away with Jake.

"No, I don't wanna play. Let's go in." The wind blew beneath the hem of my shirt, and I shivered. "Cain," I whined, "please, I'll give you a treat." At the promise of a treat, he jumped up. When we got back inside, I tossed him a beef strip from the treat bag and locked the door behind us. I started across the kitchen, but Cain sat in front of the French doors.

"Let's go." I swept my arm forward, but Cain whimpered. "What's your deal?" I took another step toward the oversized doorway leading to the foyer. Cain whimpered again and turned toward the patio, bumping his nose against the glass as though he wanted to go back out.

"No, it's time to be inside." But Cain turned in a circle, his pitiful whimper growing. Great, he must need to go. "Ugh! Why didn't you do your business when you were outside?" I stomped back to the door. Mom would kill me if he stained a rug, and I sure wasn't dying to clean up after him. Cain jumped up, leaving marks in the cream paint beside the door. "Down! What's wrong with you?" I had to use my knee to shove him away from the doorknob. Cain hadn't jumped at the door like that since he was a puppy, and Dad had broken his jumping with a vibrating collar. He nearly knocked me down as he barreled out onto the patio. I expected him to make a beeline for the corner of the yard where he usually left his little gifts, but he stopped at the edge of the rock patio and turned back to me. He growled, the 'I wanna kill something' growl he normally reserved for delivery men. I pointed my finger.

"Don't you growl at me again, stupid dog. Go. Do your thing so we can go back inside." I shooed him with a flick of my hand, but he only growled louder, the hair on his withers standing up. Goosebumps broke out on my arms that had nothing to do with the open door. I turned around quickly, but the kitchen looked exactly as it had a minute ago. I turned back to Cain, whose growl grew louder as he lowered his head.

"You're freakin' me out. Stop it." But Cain continued to growl. I mentally ran through my lockup checklist. I'd locked the deadbolt on the front door when my parents left, and I knew Mom would never leave a window unlocked. The patio door had been locked when I came down. I either had to get the dog inside and let him search the house, or I had to go out with him. When Cain's growl turned to a bark, I jumped and dashed out the door. I immediately thought of the last time he'd barked at me, the day I'd gotten the necklace, and my hand found the pendant beneath the collar of my t-shirt.

Cain immediately came to me and continued growling toward the kitchen door. My heart was pounding as sweat broke out along my back. He wasn't growling at me this time. Whatever had him upset was inside the house.

My eyes searched the semi-darkened doorway, but with the patio light glaring above me, I couldn't make out a thing. I had to get a grip. I pressed my hand against chest, brushing my fingers across the clover pendant. I fiddled with the pendant, sliding it along the chain and breathing deeply in an attempt to calm my racing pulse.

Suddenly, Cain stopped growling and bumped his nose against my hand. "Are you completely mental?" I asked, wondering if I might be the mental one. I knelt beside him, and he tried to lick my face as I massaged behind his ear. "Do we go in now?" I stood and walked back to the door, but Cain stopped at the threshold. "Not again."

Despite the fear I had of going back inside, we couldn't stay out here all night, but I wasn't about to go in without him. I'd have to lure him in. I grabbed a treat from the bag, but Cain didn't move. "Come on, boy." I shook the treat, but he stayed as though commanded.

I sniffed the beef strip and crinkled my nose. "Wouldn't work on me either." I'd need something a little more tempting. I walked slowly across the kitchen, scanning from side to side. My heart nearly jumped right out of my chest as I caught my reflection in the mirror above the table. I had to stop myself from running back outside.

This was ridiculous. I huffed out a breath and clutched at my chest again. I was letting my imagination get the better of me. I pulled open the fridge and dug around in the bottom drawer where Mom kept the lunch meat. A slice of ham ought to do it. I glanced over my shoulder where Cain had backed all the way to the edge of the patio again. Better make it two slices. I grabbed another slice and shut the fridge.

"Alright, Cain." I held the slices by my fingertips and shook them. "I've got a special treat." But Cain's hackles went up as a low rumble broke from his raised lips. "Cain! Now stop it!" The hair along my neck and arms stood up as a cold air rushed toward me. Whatever he didn't like was between us.

I stepped toward him, and he stepped toward me, barking uncontrollably. Spit flew from his mouth. The lamp and string lights flickered. I jerked my head toward the counter on my right. A gush of air to my left had me whipping in that direction where my eyes caught my reflection. The stone in the center of my pendant flashed in the light as another image materialized in the mirror.

The shape was vague at first and slowly materialized into the shape of a woman or girl. The girl was more of a gray outline than a solid image, colorless except for the eyes. Her crystal-blue eyes drew mine in the mirror, but when I jerked my head toward the kitchen, no one was there. I looked back at the mirror as a bead of sweat trailed down the center of my back. I couldn't clearly make out her face. It seemed to swirl and change constantly. She reached toward me, her mouth moving but no sound escaping. I stepped back and bumped into the counter, the ham slices falling from my hand. I glanced to Cain who'd stepped within the doorway, where he still barked fiercely.

The girl's image moved toward mine in the mirror. I held out my hand and screamed, "No!" The image swept from the mirror and materialized before me, except it was no longer just an image. Her body was more solid and less than a foot from me. I couldn't see through her though she remained that colorless gray. "No!" I tried to step to the side, but my slippers caused me to stumble, and my backside hit the kitchen tile hard. She leaned toward me, her hand reaching again as her eyes shifted from that mesmerizing blue to black. My eyes squeezed closed of their own accord. "Cain!"

I heard a flurry of claws across the tile and a scrap of something sharp against my stomach, and when I forced my eyes open, Cain was standing over me, hackles lowered and his big tongue hanging out in a pant. I scooted from under him and sat leaning back against the counter. We were alone.

CHAPTER 23

Cain turned in a circle and laid down in front of my closed bedroom door, his tongue hanging from the side of his mouth in a heavy pant. The two of us had raced up the stairs as soon as the spirit vanished. My body shook so badly that the bed bounced beneath me. I pulled my knees to my chest and slid back until my back hit the headboard, grabbed a pillow, and buried my head in it. My mind raced.

What happened wasn't possible. I didn't just see a …a what? A ghost? I couldn't have, right? It wasn't possible. A ghost did not just try to touch me. No, no, no! I slammed my head into the pillow and screamed. What was happening to me? What would have happened without Cain? Could she have killed me?

I threw the pillow across the room. Cain's ears perked, but he didn't stand. Maybe the ordeal had shaken him as badly as it had me. Tears burned the backs of my eyes. If it wasn't real, if I hadn't seen …her, then I was losing it, going completely crazy. If I had seen her, then what? I was being stalked by a ghost? The dreams, the voice, the eyes I'd seen in my mirror, it would all make sense. Was this Phillip Ezra's sister? The dream images came swirling in. I'd never seen her face in any of the dreams, but the "feel" of her was the same. When I'd faced her in the mirror and then in front of me, I'd sensed her fear as much as I'd felt my own. Fear and something else, something very much like longing. But longing for what? In all of my dreams, she'd wanted to belong, to be accepted, first by the kids at school and then by her own brother. Was that what she wanted from me?

Panic was rising inside me again. None of this was logical. My whole life was built around logic. I was safe inside my logic.

It wrapped its arms around me and protected me when life was unpredictable; it shielded me from injustice and unfairness. Without logic, anything was possible, and if anything was possible, nothing was safe. Logic was failing me. I had nothing to hold onto, no light in the dark.

I had to talk to someone, reground myself. I grabbed my phone. I'd call Mom. I unlocked my phone's screen and pushed the thumbnail of her face, but I stopped before completing the call. My finger hovered over the green phone icon. If I called her, what would I say? Hey, Mom, can you come home? I think I saw a ghost. After she heard how upset I was, I knew she'd come, but I didn't think it was fair to ruin Mom's night away. She and Dad rarely got to get away between Dad's classes and Mom's business. It sounded stupid and irrational to *me*, so I knew it would sound even worse to her, but she'd come home because I was scared. Her seventeen-year-old daughter afraid of nothing. It was nothing after all. It had to be. I'd imagined it. That was the only explanation. But that didn't stop my body from shaking or the tears I had to keep blinking back.

Calling Jake was out. No way I was going to beg him to come home after I'd been so mean to Rachel. And the only other person I could call was Rachel. So that meant it was just me and Cain, my silent partner in all this. I looked at him. His head was on his paws, his heavy, old man brows pushed together as if to ask what now. When the phone buzzed in my hand, we both jumped, and Cain sat up taller.

It buzzed again. Someone was calling me, but the screen read "Unknown" with no number beneath it. Normally, I wouldn't answer since it was typically a telemarketer, but the thought of hearing another human voice sounded great, even if she or he was trying to sell me a time-share in Branson, Missouri.

"Hello," I said.

A perky female voice answered, "Hey, Ria!"

I frowned, not recognizing the voice. "Who is this?"

"It's Dee."

Dee? I couldn't remember giving her my number, but her voice was better than a telemarketer, so I didn't question it. "Dee?"

"What're you doing? No hot date?" She giggled.

I tried to take some of the edge from voice and relax the tension inside me. "Not even close, unless you count my dog." My racing pulse was beginning to relax, and Cain lay back down. "I'm glad you called."

"Yeah, me, too. Not much happening with me tonight either. You okay? You sound a little strange."

I quickly debated on whether or not to tell Dee what had happened, but before I could speak, she continued.

"Did you see a ghost or something?" She laughed, but her insight caught me off guard, and I answered before I could think better of it.

"Yeah, I think so." Suddenly, my eyes filled again, and this time I let them spill down my cheeks. I couldn't explain the tears any more than I could explain the girl in my kitchen, and maybe I was still holding onto her longing, her fear, but I needed to tell Dee right now. I needed her to accept what I'd seen.

"Really?" Her voice had that hint of incredulous but not as much as I'd expected.

"Yeah, it—she—was in my kitchen. She came out of the mirror." I paused to hear her reaction, but the only sound coming through the phone was a rustling sound, almost like I could hear her steps in her voice. "She was all gray, except for her eyes."

"Her eyes?" she asked.

"They were blue, so blue that they almost seemed to glow. She stepped out of the mirror and reached for me."

"Like to touch you?" Again, I could hear the rustling.

I nodded even though she couldn't see me. "Yeah, she reached out her hand, and I screamed. Our dog came charging at us, then she vanished."

"Did she hurt you?" A chill made the hair on my arms stand. Dee's voice felt close, really close. Once I'd misplaced Mom in a crowded department store and had called her phone to find her. Turned out she was only ten feet behind me near a bulging rack of coats. As soon as she answered, I could somehow tell she was nearby and had immediately spun around to find her. That's how it felt with Dee in that moment as if I could spin around, and she'd be there.

I rubbed my arms. "No, she didn't hurt me."

"You should talk to her."

"Talk to her?" I wanted to laugh and not like I'd just heard a joke, more in the you-must-be-out-of-your-mind way. "I hope I never see her again." I absently brought my clover pendant to my mouth, running it along my lips.

"Why ever would you hope that?" I swear I could feel her breathy question against my cheek, and my heart started to beat faster.

At the same instant, I heard the front door open, and Rachel's laugh echoed both up the stairs and through the phone pressed to my ear. I froze, the clover dangling from my chin. I heard Rachel say, "You're so funny, Jake!" into my ear as clearly as if I'd been standing in the foyer beside them.

Dee was calling from inside my house.

Leaping from the bed with my phone still in my hand, I flung open the door and bounded down the hall. From the top of the stairs, I saw Jake kicking off his shoes. Rachel was pushing against his arm, trying to knock him off-balance. Jake glanced up, the smile still on his face until he saw me.

He glared at me, but at that moment, I didn't care. Even his glare was a welcome sight since it meant I wasn't alone. I looked all around the foyer and leaned over to see into the kitchen doorway. My heart pounded, and my hand shook as I held up my phone, but the screen was blank, my phone dark. I pushed the home button and slid my finger over the sensor, but when it lit up, I was back on my home screen. A touch revealed that I'd had no recent calls. Had I dreamed Dee's call?

Cain trotted past me without so much as a look and down the stairs to greet Jake with a loud bark, his tail beating fiercely against Rachel's leg. Jake scratched behind his left ear, and he turned for the family room without speaking to me.

Rachel, whose eyes hadn't left me, gave a sad half-smile, and she followed Jake, leaving me there with a sick feeling in my stomach.

CHAPTER 24

The next few days were a blur. I tried to dismiss what I'd heard, what I'd seen, but the memory gnawed at me like Cain with a bone. One minute I was certain I'd seen a spirit and heard Dee's voice, but the next my logical mind refused to let me accept any of it.

As soon as I went back upstairs that night, I checked my call log again, but it showed no recent activity. I still couldn't remember giving her my number, which would fit with my having imagined the entire phone call, but that didn't explain what I'd experienced in the kitchen. I had no proof, other than my memory, making it all so much worse. If I had dreamed up this entire episode, what did that say about my mental state? It was exactly like the mysterious text I'd tried to show Mom. No evidence meant it hadn't happened.

I spent the entire night huddled under my covers with my lamp on. When Mom and Dad came home late the next day, I couldn't find the words to explain what had happened. If I doubted myself, how could I ever explain it to them? No normal person would believe me. None of this made sense.

So, I pretended. I pretended I was normal, that a spirit had not appeared to me, that Cain hadn't rescued me, and that I wasn't losing my mind. I went to school. I came home. I tried to study, but every night, I stayed awake for hours, waiting for her to reappear.

Every noise made me jump. If Mom knocked on my door to put away clothes, my heart raced for thirty minutes afterward. If Dad tried to ask me about school, I could only reply with a standard, "It was fine." I was afraid if I said more than that, I wouldn't be able to keep my story buried inside, and the words would come spilling out like an overflowing sink.

I didn't talk to Jake even when he drove us to school. He'd stopped texting to let me know when practice was over. I'd just wait by his truck until he showed up, Rachel on his arm, and I'd climb in the back seat, my new unofficial location since Rachel had started riding to and from school with us. Rachel gave me that same sad-eyed look each day, but I didn't talk to her for the same reason I didn't talk to Mom or Dad. It was the most difficult fifteen minutes of my day, riding to and from school with two people whom I loved very much but couldn't bring myself to apologize to.

Every time I glanced in the mirror, the necklace I'd been wearing for weeks stared back at me. None of these things had happened before I'd put on that necklace. The dreams, the text, the spirit—it was all connected, but when I tried to take the necklace off, I still couldn't budge the clasp. Desperate, I'd yanked on it until I bruised the back of my neck, but the chain wouldn't break. The necklace had a hold on me; it wasn't letting go any time soon. And a small part of me wanted to get to the bottom of it all. Every time I touched the clover, I remembered my dream about Phillip Ezra, the way he'd wanted to make his sister feel loved, and the fear of the girl that I now assumed had to be his sister. I still didn't know her name, but I would make it my mission to learn her identity. Soon.

****

The beeping of the intercom interrupted the quiet of AP physics. "Teachers, at this time we'll go to the assembly. Please take your classes to the gym."

I'd forgotten about the assembly this afternoon along with the quiz I'd just been fumbling my way through. Everyone else stood noisily, excited to be out of class for the next hour, but my test was only two-thirds completed, and Ms. Jordan's eyes met mine immediately.

"It's okay, Ria. Finish your quiz." She stepped through the doorway after the last student, and I could hear her telling the teacher next door that she'd be there when I was done.

When she came back, I said, "Sorry."

The smile across her face clearly showed she wasn't sorry to be missing Michael Gideon's performance. "Are you kidding? I should be thanking you for saving me from the headache that was bound to come from all that." She gestured toward the direction of the door. "I dread it every year."

Michael Gideon was a regular at Thomasville High. Last year, Rachel told me they'd practically watched the man's hair turn gray since elementary school. Every year, he came to karaoke and brought his 'anti-drug' message that they'd all loved as munchkins but which had grown a little sad as they'd matured. He must have been a wannabe musician in his youth who'd turned his unsuccessful attempts at breaking into the industry into a 180-day gig around the nation as a single-man public service announcement. But every year, the administration still booked him.

I stared at the three questions I hadn't answered, the equations seemingly defying logic. Had I really fallen this far behind? I hadn't realized how far my distraction had gone. Not only was I losing sleep, but now my grades were suffering as well, and I still wasn't any closer into finding out who Phillip Ezra's sister was. I hadn't even figured out who to ask. Control was slipping away, and I felt the familiar panic rising as it had in Coach Joseph's class. The words on the page blurred as tears filled my eyes, and my breath came quicker.

I must have made a noise because Ms. Jordan said, "What's wrong?"

I tried to swallow past the fist jammed in my throat and answer her, but my mouth opened and closed like a dying goldfish. She rose from her chair and came around beside me, squatting down next to me.

"Hey, what's going on with you lately? The past few weeks you haven't been yourself at all."

I shook my head and swiped at my eyes, glad I hadn't been bothering with makeup since Saturday night. At least I wouldn't have raccoon eyes. "I don't ...I just..." How could I tell my favorite teacher I thought I was losing my mind. "I haven't been sleeping well." Or at all.

She patted my arm, then the quiz. "I'll tell you what. I know you have bonuses. Why don't you turn them in?"

Ms. Jordan gave bonus points for homework completion. I had seven, but she normally only accepted them on big tests. For her to offer to take them on just a quiz, she must have realized how close to my breaking point I was. "But it's only a quiz," I reminded her.

"I won't tell if you won't," she said, rising. "Now you dig them out."

I nodded and opened the small zipper compartment on my bag, taking out the folded papers and smoothing them out. She took the quiz and the papers back to her desk. "Just don't show anyone your quiz when you get it back." She motioned toward the door with a bob of her head. "You go on to the shindig, and I'll be right behind you—maybe."

At her mischievous grin, I gave a small smile. "I won't tell if you won't."

I heard the assembly before I actually opened the metal door leading inside. Mr. Shiloh stood sentry outside, checking his phone messages. He raised his brows at me.

"I was finishing a quiz," I said in answer to his silent

question. I didn't mention physics, so I wouldn't be selling out Ms. Jordan's absence at the assembly. He nodded and moved to open the door.

"Missed your family at church Sunday."

I shrugged. The last thing I wanted to talk about was my surreal Saturday night experience. "Mom and Dad were out of town, and I stayed home to study." Lying about church—I was going straight to Hell for that one.

"Saw Jake with Rachel." He raised his brows again. "Something going on there?"

Mr. Shiloh was notoriously nosey. He could gossip with the best of them, asking questions under the guise of 'need to know' for school climate, but really, he was plain nosey.

"You'll have to ask them that." I shrugged.

With raised brows, he grunted and opened the door for me. After sliding past him, I went into the gym. With only the gel lights set up for the party atmosphere, I could barely see. Kids were on their feet waving their arms and dancing along to a popular song turned up so loudly I couldn't even have heard my own voice. The girls were smashed together swaying and bumping, their mouths moving along with the lyrics while the jocks shoved and rough-housed jovially, everyone seemingly glad to have a brief reprieve from class. In the distant, truly dark corners were those kids who could care less, those determined not to enjoy themselves no matter what. Some were so close they had to be doing more than just holding hands. Teachers were sitting against the wall or in folding chairs on the fringe of the performance. A couple of the more adventurous faculty members were dancing with the kids and singing, most looked as though they'd rather have a root canal than be sitting there.

After scanning the bleachers, I moved to sit on the far end where I could hide in the shadows until it ended. I didn't bother to look for Rachel or Jake. Neither would want me to sit with them. I squeezed into the corner, adjusting my messenger bag beside me and thinking about the quiz I was certain I'd just failed, but when I glanced toward the double doors not far from the bleachers, the laser lights flashed around the area, and for a second, they lit up Dee's face. She was looking at me and waving from where she stood beside a set of double doors that led to a small hallway off the gym. I needed to talk to Dee, see if she had called me Saturday or if I'd imagined it all.

Grabbing my bag, I started back down the bleachers and saw her open the door just wide enough to slip out. I figured she wanted to talk in the hall or maybe sneak away from the madness of the gym. Glancing back over her shoulder to make sure I was following, she let the door shut behind her, assumedly to keep from attracting the attention of the teachers sitting about fifteen feet in front of the door. I followed her out, blinking against the brightness of the hallway. But she wasn't there. To the right, the hallway dead-ended, so I turned left and followed it past a set of restrooms. Sticking my head inside the restroom, I called her name. There were only two stalls, and no feet were under the doors. She couldn't have gone far. Letting the door close behind me, I turned to continue down the hall when I heard the voice I'd been living with for weeks.

"Free me, Ria."

The sibilant sound carried down the hall as though it were just ahead. The hair on my arms lifted, and a chill swept up my spine. I knew if I kept walking I would find something; I didn't know what, but every nerve in my body was screaming there was something down that hall.

"Ria," the voice seemed to confirm my intuition. *She* wanted me there, but I wasn't sure I wanted to go. The last few days had cemented both my desire to be free of all this and my need to know more. I was torn between wanting to run and craving the truth.

"Ria!"

This time the voice was directly over my shoulder, and the ceiling lights behind me went dark.

CHAPTER 25

Fear forced my feet to run. Without conscious thought, I bolted forward down the part of the hallway that was still lit then deeper into the bowels of the gym. Clutching the strap of my bag as though it were a lifeline, I ran. The hall twisted past closed doors, and the floor changed from white tile to dingy cement as I came to a ramp of sorts. My speed increased on the slanting floor, and I tripped over my own feet, falling and sliding to a stop against the unyielding cement. I sat up slowly and lifted my hands close to my face to assess the damage.

Scrapes on the heels of my palms welled with blood, but pain in my knee quickly overtook any concern I had with my hands. Looking down at the tear in the right leg of my jeans, I could see an angry scrape at least an inch long on the skin beneath my kneecap. Gingerly, I lifted my pant leg and blood ran from the abrasion. I searched my bag for a tissue and wiped it off then pressed down to stop the bleeding, wincing against the sharp pain. I normally kept a few Band-Aids in my bag, and I unwrapped two and covered the wound until I could properly tend to it later.

Pulling my pant leg back down, I stood, inhaling against the stinging ache and adjusting my bag back into place. I felt ridiculous. I'd run from a voice that was probably all in my head. I glanced around at the part of the hall where I'd landed. There were two doors to my right and one farther down on the left.

Something about the hall felt familiar although I was positive I'd never been to this part of the gym. A biting cold seeped through my cardigan and t-shirt. The air felt damp and smelled musty, that earthy smell like a basement. The cool surface temporarily eased the stinging of my scraped palm when I rested it against the wall.

"Ria."

The voice was coming from the doorway on the left down the hall. The door was open. It was stupid and a classic scary movie move, but I had to know. The skin across my knee tightened as I walked tentatively toward the doorway. The open door was metal and dark with a handle that pushed down instead of a knob. I put my hand against the chipped paint as I stepped inside the room.

A small window high on the wall showed a rectangular section of gray autumn sky met by wilted grass and confirmed I was in a basement. To my left, a black boiler sat like an angry monster. I could tell by the lack of heat or glowing light that the boiler was no longer in use, replaced years ago by heating units outside the gym.

Like the hall, the room was familiar and foreign at the same time. I turned in a circle, trying to place it in my memory and walking farther. I was looking up at the dirty window when the door slammed. I heard a click as though a lock had been turned.

Rushing to the door, I tried the handle, but it wouldn't turn. I yanked, but the door wouldn't budge.

"Hey! Open this door!" I yelled as panic quickened my pulse. The scratches on my palms burned as I pounded and screamed.

The overhead light went out, leaving me in semi-darkness with only the weak fall sunlight of the small window. I flicked the wall switch on and off, but nothing happened.

Pressing my back against the door, I slid down the cool surface as spots danced in my vision. I was hyperventilating, but I couldn't stop myself. I tried to concentrate on the tear in my jeans, the dirt on the cuff of my pink cardigan, but nothing was working, and I curled against the door, unable to stop the darkness from coming for me.

****

"Please stay away from me, Bart. I just want to be left alone." I feel the tears in my eyes, and I know he can see them, but he doesn't care.

"Aw, she's upset—again," Bart taunts me. "Gonna tell big brother?" He laughs and flips on the light.

I blink against the brightness, and Phoebe laughs as she hangs on his arm. Her maroon cheerleading uniform strains against her curves, and her blonde ponytail bounces every time she laughs. Bart pulls away from her and adjusts his letterman's jacket as he kneels next to me. He leans in close, the raised "T" on his jacket rubs against my arm as he whispers in my ear.

"Phillip got me called into Coach's office over you. Told Coach he would kick my ass next time I messed with you." He touches my cheek with one finger. "You should've just gone out with me, and none of this would've happened."

I scoot back away from his hand. The smell of his cologne is making my stomach turn. "You have Phoebe. You don't need another girl."

Bart glances up at Phoebe, then back down at me. "Everyone has Phoebe."

Phoebe gasps. "You take that back!"

Bart rubs Phoebe's calf and slides his hand up the back of it, but she slaps it away and crosses her arms over her chest. "You know it's true, babe, and you're not gonna break up with me because, well, I'm the last guy left on the team that'll have you—except for Paul." He motions toward the door where I see Paul slink inside, hands jammed in the pockets of his letterman's jacket. "You haven't dated him yet."

Paul pushes his red hair out of his eyes and smirks. "Not likely.

I wouldn't touch her with your—"

Phoebe smacks him on the chest and arms. He laughs again and grabs her wrists. "Enough." He drops her wrists, and Phoebe stomps outside the room. I can hear her footsteps echoing down the hall. "Let's go, Bart. We got a party to get to." Paul turns and disappears out the door.

Bart stands. "Yeah, guess you're right." He pauses in the doorway and looks back at me. "But don't worry. I'll see you again soon, Delilah."

CHAPTER 26

I opened my eyes and sat up in one motion, which made the room swirl around me until I regained my equilibrium. I glanced at my watch. It was 2:30. I'd been down here for over an hour. I jumped up and grabbed the door handle. That's when I remembered. I'd been locked in, and the lights had been off. I looked up at the light, which was clearly on. I turned the handle and easily pulled the door open.

Sweat dotted my forehead. Had I had another panic attack and imagined it all? The dream tumbled back to me. Bart, Paul, Phoebe …Delilah. The girl's name was Delilah. The spirit had been a girl named Delilah. And she'd been tormented by Bart Joseph, my brother's coach and my teacher.

My phone buzzed from my bag. I fumbled inside until I found it and saw Jake's goofy grin on the screen. Jake hadn't talked to me in days, but he was calling now.

"Hello?" I said, walking out of the room and jogging down the hall.

"Where are you?" he asked, irritation edging his voice.

"I'm on my way to class." I deliberately avoided telling him what I'd been doing or where I was because I wasn't sure what to say.

"I'm in the office. When you didn't show up to class, they called me in to see if I could reach you."

I could hear a voice in the background asking for the phone, then Mr. Shiloh said, "Ria, where have you been? You missed sixth hour."

"I'm sorry, Mr. Shiloh. I'm on my way now." I rushed up the ramp and back down the hall toward the gym door I'd sneaked out of earlier following Dee. Had she even been there at all? Had I imagined her as well?

The thought brought me to a stop. Dee. I remembered all the times we'd been together—the study session where we'd met, the gym during the football game, the coffee shop. The strange looks from the barista when I'd ordered two coffees and the women in the stadium lobby when Dee and I had been making plans, the vintage clothes and jewelry so like Delilah's in my visions, the fact that she didn't want to be touched. No one but I had ever interacted with Dee. No one knew her, had any idea who she was. My spirit girl had been named Delilah. It didn't take calculus to add up the connection, and I felt completely stupid for not having seen the obvious before now. Delilah was Dee. I'd been talking to a dead girl all along.

"Ria? Are you still there?" Mr. Shiloh's voice was beyond irritated.

"Yes, sir. I'm crossing the gym now." I hurried past Michael Gideon where he rolled up cables and put them inside black trunks. By the looks of it, he'd been finished for a while.

"Come to my office immediately."

Without giving me a chance to say anything else, Mr. Shiloh disconnected the call. I was in big trouble.

CHAPTER 27

My mind still swirling with thoughts of Delilah, I opened the glass door leading into the office. The secretary eyed me over the top of her glasses and said, "Go on in."

I nodded and went into Mr. Shiloh's office, closing the door behind me. Mr. Shiloh was behind the desk, and Coach Joseph was standing next to it, pointing down at something on the desk.

Seeing the two of them together brought the boiler room dream back to me. I glanced at Mr. Shiloh's name plate on his desk—Mr. Paul Shiloh. *"I'm the last guy left on the team that'll have you—except for Paul."* The red-headed boy from the dream was Paul Shiloh, my principal.

Coach looked up from the paper on the desk and over at me, his eyes narrowed as he watched me from across the room. "Are you alright, Ria?"

I nodded, my mouth dry. These two had harassed a teenage girl, had chased her into the dark and bullied her, maybe worse than that. After all, I'd only seen a couple of dreams. What else had they done to her that she hadn't yet shown me?

Mr. Shiloh handed the paper back to Coach. "I think that'll be fine, Bart. Just have the boys sign out before they go pick up the shirts."

Coach nodded and folded the paper. "I'll tell them." He gave a half-smile to me as he turned toward the door.

Mr. Shiloh sat back in his padded leather chair. He automatically smoothed the pale red ring of hair at the back of his head and tugged down his blue tie over his pudgy midsection. The years had clearly not been kind to Mr. Shiloh, but he didn't seem to have been too kind back then. Maybe he deserved it.

I couldn't believe this was the same guy who'd been so cruel to Delilah. This was the guy who sat near the front of my church every Sunday, but then again, didn't Coach do that, too?

"Where were you? You missed history, which means you were truant. Do you know what the punishment for that is?" He reached behind him and took a student policy booklet from a short bookshelf then handed it to me. "Page seventy-two."

I flipped to page seventy-two and read the truancy policy. According to the handbook, I could be placed in in-school suspension for "skipping" class. I closed the booklet and placed it on his desk.

"I'm sorry, Mr. Shiloh." I almost choked on his name. Paul Shiloh had been part of what had happened to Delilah Ezra. Bullying seemed like a minor term for being chased into a basement by two boys the size of Jake. "I had a headache and went to the restroom beside the gym to try to wait out the show. I must have fallen asleep. I woke up sitting on the floor." The lie seemed believable enough. I held his gaze in hopes he believed I'd simply slept through the assembly and sixth hour.

He sighed. "You're a good student, but recently I've heard some disturbing things. Coach told me about your episode in his class, and Nurse Tadmor said you insisted on sitting in her office instead of returning to class. Your behavior is beginning to concern me."

I looked at my hands, trying to appear contrite even though I felt like I didn't owe him any explanation. I was seeing visions because of something that happened to Delilah, and he was part of that something. I didn't care that he was the principal. A leopard can't change its spots. On the outside, he might be the responsible guardian to an entire building of students, but inside he was still the same hateful bully. It wasn't fair that his outside didn't reflect that. It wasn't fair that everyone thought he was this wonderful, caring man, the oil in the gears in our high school that kept it running smoothly.

"I'm going to call your mother and let her know what happened, and if I hear about one more problem, Ria, I'll have no choice but to punish you. Understood?"

I nodded before going to seventh hour, not bothering to thank him. I was afraid if I opened my mouth my true feelings about him would tumble out. No, I couldn't let him know that I knew the real Paul Shiloh and Bart Joseph. I would hold it all inside until I figured out how best to use what I knew. I glanced over my shoulder before I closed his office door, and disgust boiled inside of me.

My pulse raced but not from fear this time. I gripped the strap of my messenger bag to stop the angry tremors in my hands as I passed Coach Joseph's closed door. I would find a way to bring out the truth of their cruelty. I would show everyone they weren't the church-going good guys they showed themselves to be.

In my mind, I could see Delilah, ruined pink dress and all, sitting in that filthy boiler room floor, except this time, Dee's face stared back at me, dark curls cupping her tear-dampened cheeks. "Free me, Ria,"ghosted through my mind as her mouth moved with the words.

And this time, I nodded.

CHAPTER 28

During the ride home from school, Jake didn't bother to ask me about what had happened, but I caught him glancing at me several times in the rear-view mirror. Rachel, looking as though she would burst, chewed her nails and even turned around once like she was going to ask before quickly spinning back to face the front.

For the last hour, the vision of Delilah's—Dee's—eyes had tortured me. And with each minute my anger bubbled until I was in full rage mode with no idea what to do about it. I had to get even with them for Dee's sake. That's what she'd been trying to tell me all along, but I didn't really know how to do that, so my anger had nowhere to go. I could feel it in the tightness of my shoulders and the headache pulsing behind my ears. Closing my eyes, I rolled my neck.

All I wanted was the solitude of my room to think. Delilah needed something from me. She needed my help, but I wasn't sure how to go about it. I also needed to know what had happened to her. She felt trapped, or she wouldn't be pleading for me to free her, but why was she trapped? What happened after the visions she'd shown me?

If only she would point me in the right direction. I couldn't believe I was actually hoping for another visit from her. She'd scared the crap out of me the last time, but that's the only way I could see what she needed.

How had my life changed so quickly? A few weeks ago, I didn't even want to watch a scary movie; now, I was wishing for contact from a dead girl? But I needed to know the rest of her story, to see what had happened to the pretty girl with the sad eyes. I slid the clover pendant along its chain, anxious to be out of Jake's truck. The necklace had connected Delilah and me. Maybe I could use it to reach out to her.

I hopped out of the truck before Jake could even put it in park and rushed up the walk, planning to run upstairs, ignore the homework in my bag, and Google how to contact a ghost, but as soon as I opened the front door, Mom called me into the kitchen.

"Alright, spill." She was standing with her hands on her hips and her brows nearly touching from the scowl on her face. Her blonde curls were frizzy like she'd been running her hands through it.

"It's nothing. I have a headache." I rubbed my temples as much from necessity as for affect. "I went to the bathroom to avoid the worst of the noise during that asinine show, and I fell asleep. You know I haven't been sleeping well. I guess I was more tired than I thought." I sighed, and it wasn't just part of a pity act to get out of trouble. "So, I got yelled at by the principal, missed important class notes that I need to copy off tonight, ripped my jeans and, oh yeah,—" some of my anger spilled out in my tone, but I couldn't make myself care "—likely failed a physics quiz. It's been a terrible day, Mom." I let my shoulders sag and felt some fleeting relief from the tension in them.

Mom shook her head and looked down at the floor before turning her back to me. She went to the cabinet and shook out two ibuprofens from the plastic bottle inside. She turned back to me and took my hand from where I gripped my messenger bag, dropping the tiny, brown pills inside it before going to the fridge for a cola. Popping the top, she brought it back to me.

"Take those, drink that, and go lie down. I'll call you when supper's ready, then you can do your homework if your headache is gone." She leaned in and kissed my cheek. She smelled like fabric softener and home, and I felt my anger slipping away. In its wake, tears burned my eyes and tightened my throat. I wanted to tell her everything about Delilah and the visions and how damn angry I'd felt in Mr. Shiloh's office, but I couldn't. She'd think I was losing my mind, and I was afraid she'd be right. I just couldn't say it aloud, not yet, not till I knew more about what had happened to Delilah Ezra, and the only way to do that was to somehow communicate with her.

I put the pills in my mouth and swallowed them with a big gulp of soda before setting the can back on the counter. Mom nodded, then pulled me to her for a hug.

With her hands still on my shoulders, she said, "I love you, Miriam. I know what happened today was not you being you. You're tired and stressed, and I don't know how to help you."

"I'm fine, really, and I'm sorry about today. It won't happen again." I started to walk around her when she gently grabbed my arm.

"I'm here. You know that, right? I love you, and I don't expect anything of you. You have to stop putting so much pressure on yourself." Her blue eyes pleaded with me, but my anger surged back full-force.

Pressure? She didn't have a clue. She could say she didn't expect anything, but how would she feel if I came home with an 'F'? Bet she'd do more than just give me a soda and tell me to rest. What did she know about being me? She couldn't possibly understand what it was like to be a teenager in today's society. She'd never taken an AP class or lived in the shadow of her popular, athletic brother, not to mention dealing with the drama social media created on a daily basis. In that moment, I couldn't stand to look at her. She didn't understand the pressure her perfect life put on me. How did she expect me to ever live up to what she'd done? Creating a successful business, managing a family, looking and acting so perfect all of the time?

I shook my head, trying to dissipate the building anger. My mother had never been anything but good to me. She'd always encouraged me to be happy, had never forced me to be more than I was. But fight as I may, the fury in me was winning, and all I could do was clamp my lips down tightly to avoid saying something I'd later regret.

I forced a nod and headed to my room. When I glanced inside the family room, Jake was sitting on the couch. I knew Rachel would be on the floor between the couch and coffee table, her books and notebook spread out before her, just like they did every night now. He leaned forward and disappeared from view for a second, and from the sound of her high-pitched squeal, I assumed he was tickling her, probably somewhere I didn't want to know about. Gag.

I couldn't stand their happiness. He'd stolen my best friend from me to add to his trophy room of girls, and he'd dump her just like the rest, then she'd be out of both of our lives. The only difference would be he'd move on, and I'd be friendless. I hated him, and I hated her for ever wanting to date Jake in the first place. I hated them both for their happiness and their easy-going relationship.

Some non-fuming part of my brain tried to remind me that I'd caused the chasm between Rachel and me. I'd been ugly and mean and said terrible things to her, but that part of me was quickly silenced, and for a second, I had the irrational urge to hurt them both, and not in the emotional way I had before. White-hot fury made my whole body shake.

As his head reappeared over the top of the couch and her squeals turned to delighted giggles, I wanted nothing more than to grab a handful of his curls, yank his head back, and see how many times I could punch his smug face before he could stop me. I wanted to smash her head against that coffee table and see how much he liked her after her pretty face was gone.

As though he could feel my malevolent thoughts, he turned and looked at me, his eyes locking with mine. When we were little, people often asked if we were twins because we were so close in age, and we would sometimes pretend we were and that we had that twin sense, that we could feel what the other felt and read each other's thoughts. When he looked at me right then, I felt like he could see into my mind, could hear my dark thoughts as though I'd said them aloud. Whatever he saw in my face wrinkled his forehead. He tilted his head and stared hard, not with anger but with something else, something that looked a lot like concern, and that look punched me in the gut.

For what felt like the millionth time today, tears filled my eyes, and the sob in my throat broke loose. He angled his body more toward me, turning as far as the couch would allow and putting his arm on the back, never breaking the hold with my eyes. Chest heaving and shoulders shaking, I let the anger morph into whatever this was, and the tears came rapid fire. I'd just imagined physically hurting my brother for no reason other than he was happy. I'd skipped class and failed a test. One minute I was so angry I was consumed; the next, I was sobbing.

Dear Lord, what was happening to me?

"Ria?" Jake's face was blurred by my tears, but the worry was clear in his voice. Other than the call he'd been forced to make today, he hadn't spoken to me since I'd been so ugly to Rachel, but now his voice was like it had been when we used to be close, when we played and laughed for hours on end. This was Bub, not Jake, and it broke something in me to hear it.

Without responding, I ran up the stairs and into my room.

PART II

1 JOHN 4:1
BELOVED, BELIEVE NOT EVERY SPIRIT.

CHAPTER 29

I leaned against my closed bedroom door, taking deep breaths to stop the shaking and tears and grinding the heels of my hands into my eyes. I couldn't explain the anger any more than I could explain how I was seeing and interacting with Delilah, and I wondered if my anger was her anger. Was I feeling so angry because Delilah had felt that way?

Tossing my bag to the floor, I went to my desk and grabbed my laptop. Turning on the lamp, I got comfortable on my bed with my laptop on my folded legs, careful not to bump my scratched knee, and searched ghosts first. I literally got 150 million hits, everything from movie reviews to doctored photographs showing images even more frightening than my personal encounter with Delilah in the kitchen.

I narrowed my search to contacting ghosts. Some of the results showed 'easy steps' for talking to the dead and were just ridiculous. Some were links to websites where mediums offered their services for a small fee, which probably meant a big fee since they didn't list the amount. Ouija boards were absolutely out. I'd seen too many movies to try that one. And, of course, I could contact one of the thousands of ghost hunting groups if I agreed to let them film their encounters. None of it seemed helpful.

Disgusted, I closed my computer and leaned back against the pillows, letting go of some of the tension. The visions had started with the pendant, the one given to Delilah by her brother because he loved her. It was a connection to her born out of his love. Maybe the pendant would help me.

I hadn't tried to remove the pendant recently. At times, I'd been so wrapped up in what was happening that I hadn't thought about it. Then after the dream about Philip, I hadn't wanted to remove it. It embodied kindness, and I could feel his love inside of it. I gripped the clover tightly in my hand and felt the prongs prick into my palm. I looked down at the indentations left in hand by the pendant's prongs and remembered the day the prongs had cut my lip. The same day the necklace refused to be removed. That couldn't be a coincidence. Had I connected with her through my blood? It sounded like a creepy movie you rented on Halloween, but it's all I had to go on.

I opened my computer and searched again, and sure enough, over a million hits came up for contacting spirits with blood. I didn't bother to read too many because frankly the posts scared me. My Baptist upbringing made me uncomfortable with the number of times 'demon' and 'Satan' appeared, and it didn't take me long to end my search and close my laptop. My entire life I'd been taught to steer clear of anything remotely related to that sort of thing.

I had inadvertently linked myself to a dead girl with an object that had meant a great deal to her. I'd been given this necklace by a stranger who couldn't remember buying it for me. Ruth Claudia had a completely different version of that day at Jonathan Ezra's estate sale. Delilah had chosen me.

I didn't want to think the word. I didn't want to contemplate the truth of it. But I couldn't stop it from invading my brain and leaving me shaking.

Possession.

Delilah had to have possessed Ms. Claudia and caused her buy the pendant for me. Did that mean she'd possessed me, too? If I was feeling what she might have felt, seeing what she'd seen, did that mean—I wouldn't allow myself to finish the thought. No. No way. It wasn't possible.

The idea of not being in control of yourself, of being taken over by someone—thing—else scared me beyond words. I'd always avoided TV shows and movies about that phenomenon. I even felt uncomfortable reading the Bible verses connected to it or even when someone dressed as a devil with red horns and a pitchfork. And now there was a very real chance I'd had a brush with it.

My heart beat faster when I suddenly remembered my unbelievable anger today, the thoughts of hurting Jake and Rachel, my resentment at my mom. I suspected I hadn't been wrong when I wondered if my anger was her anger.

I had to face the horrifying possibility that she was inside of me. My breathing increased with a panic that broke out in a sweat across my forehead. My stomach pitched, and I ran to my bathroom just in time. I heaved until my stomach was empty of the little I'd eaten. And I stood there dry heaving, wishing I could rid myself of all I'd seen as easily.

I slid down in front of the toilet and let my cheek rest against the cool tile. I had a feeling not even removing the necklace would get rid of her at this point. And as frightened as I was, I couldn't deny the pity I still felt for Delilah Ezra. I gripped the necklace again and squeezed my eyes closed.

"Free me, Ria." Dee's voice wasn't in my head this time. It came from my room.

Though the mirror wasn't turned toward the bathroom, I could still see the reflective surface from the side when I sat up. A mist covered the glass, like the bathroom mirror when I showered.

I walked into my room and stood in front of the mirror where the mist swirled and moved like smoke. I touched the glass with the tip of my left index finger. It was cold, icy cold, and the smoke swirled as though reacting to my touch. When I slid my finger across the surface, the smoke followed. A gray hand flattened against the glass with a suddenness that caused me to jerk my finger away and stumble back.

"Don't be afraid. I won't hurt you." As she spoke, she appeared in the mirror, gray but more solid than when she'd shown herself in the kitchen mirror. This time her face was that of Dee's, her eyes still that unearthly blue. The smoke swirled where her body should be, making it impossible to see any details, but her face and the hand still pressed to the glass were absolutely clear.

My feet didn't want to obey at first, but I forced myself closer once again and pressed my left hand fully to hers. The cold seeped into me, and a tendril of mist left the mirror and twirled hungrily around my fingers, passing through the gaps between them to connect her hand more completely to mine. With each brush of the mist, a fluttering ran along my arm and across my chest.

Her soft smile spoke of sadness. "I used the old woman to get to you because I knew you'd understand. You'd help me escape."

"Escape what, Dee? I don't know what you want from me." As I spoke, the tendrils grew larger and more numerous. One became two then three before combining to become thicker, moving faster. The glow of her eyes became brighter than the lamp beside the bed.

"Let me show you." The mist swirled faster, covering her face now. The blue light suffused the entire mirror as the mist moved farther up my arm, twirling around it all the way to my elbow. Cold like I'd never felt made me shake. I could hear my mother calling my name downstairs.

The sound of my mom and self-preservation flooded me with adrenaline. Rational thought popped whatever bubble had kept me connected to the glass. I tried to pull my hand back, but it wouldn't budge. I grasped my left wrist with my right hand and pulled with all my strength. But the mist pulled back. Panicked, I pulled, planting my feet and yanking, but the mist kept me anchored to the glass.

Steps bounded up the stairs down the hall. Only Jake made that much noise jogging up the stairs. The mist completely encircled my upper body, in a swirling tornado.

Jake's steps came closer to my door. Mom must have assumed I was sleeping and sent him up to bring me down for supper despite (or maybe because) we'd been fighting recently.

He knocked loudly. "Wake up. It's time to eat."

The mist swirled around my head and tugged me closer to the glass. I was losing this struggle. My head was so close to the mirror that my nose almost brushed against it. I couldn't let him see this. I didn't want him to come in and find me fighting my mirror. Dee wouldn't let him see the truth, and I'd just look even crazier, even more out of control than I already seemed.

I must have made a noise of struggle because Jake, a slight panic in his voice, called out to me again. "Ria?" He tried the knob. I knew I hadn't locked it earlier, but it refused to yield. He tugged harder. "Ria!"

I put both hands against the mirror in an attempt to push myself away from it, but the mist only tightened now that it had both of my hands. I couldn't let my face touch it. Something inside shouted not to let my head come in contact with the surface. Suddenly, it didn't matter what Jake saw or didn't see. I couldn't fight the mist any longer, and I screamed.

Jake burst into the room at the same time my head hit the mirror. The glass shattered, and the mist released me as forcefully as it had held me, pushing me backward, like letting go in tug-of-war. I fell hard onto my backside, my head bouncing against the hardwood floor.

A bleary image of Jake's face appeared above me right before everything went dark.

CHAPTER 30

I don't want to *lift my head. I can't let them see what they are doing to me. Philip said he'd take care of it, but he can't control this gang of girls. He can talk to Bart and Paul, force them to leave me alone, but he can't do that with them, or he'd be just as bad as Bart and Paul.*

Her laughter makes me cringe. When she steps closer, I scoot farther down the bench until there's no more bench left, and I'm forced to stop.

"I said look at me, skank." She bends until her head is even with mine, and I finally look at her. "He doesn't really like you, and you're completely pathetic to think he does."

"I didn't say that, Phoebe. I never said that. I don't want anything to do with him. You can have him." Her blonde hair smells like hairspray, cigarettes, and perfume. Her fluorescent green bra stands out against her unnaturally tan skin.

"You hear that, girls? I can have him," Phoebe sneers, turning to look around the locker room at her friends. "She's giving him to me." Their laughter jars through me.

"You know what I think, Delilah—" she draws out my name in a singsong way and tucks a chunk of my hair behind my ear "—your mother must have been as big a whore as you are because there is no way Philip is your full brother." She laughs again and stands. "I mean, how can someone so fine be related to a waste of space like you?"

She walks to her locker and pulls out her p.e. shirt, pulling it over her head before turning to her friends again. "You know what I would do if I were Philip? I'd put a pillow over her face while she slept, so I'd never have the embarrassment of her as my sister again."

Her friends laugh. One puts her foot next to me on the bench and ties her tennis shoe.

Phoebe snaps her fingers. "Better yet you should just go to your house and do it for him, save him the trouble. I'll bet no one would even notice for a while." She wraps her pink scrunchie around her index finger and pulls it tight. "I wonder if you tie enough of these together if you could actually use it as a rope?"

Tears that I'd sworn I'd never shed in front of her again spill over.

"Aw, are you crying?" She looks around. "I think I hurt her feelings, girls. What should I do ab—"

"Tadmor!" Coach Aaron's unmistakable voice booms across the locker room. She is standing near the door, impatience all over her face. "Get your butt out on the court right now, and since you have enough energy to tease Delilah, you can get the volleyballs out, too."

The girls file past me—all but Phoebe.

"Do us all a favor and just get it over with." She pats my head and walks out.

CHAPTER 31

"She's coming around." My mother's voice pierced the fog of my brain.

"Here, Mrs. Gabriel." Rachel? I tried to open my eyes.

A cold cloth pressed against one cheek, then the other.

"Should I call 911, Mom?" Jake sounded so upset, and I turned my head toward his voice. I cracked my eyelids, and a fuzzy face appeared close to mine but not Jake's.

Mom's blue eyes held both worry and relief. "What do you think, Isaac?"

Dad leaned in closer. "Ria, can you sit up?" He slid his arm under my shoulders and didn't wait for my response before lifting gently up.

I grabbed onto his bicep as a wave of dizziness hit like an avalanche. He stilled until I nodded, then continued to lift me up until I was sitting. My head felt like it weighed a ton, and I let it fall onto my dad's shoulder.

I looked up at my brother, careful to move only my eyes. He held up his phone and shook it a little, asking whether he should make the call or not.

"No, I think she's okay. Help me get her to her bed, son."

Jake handed his phone to Rachel and bent to slide an arm under my knees and replaced Dad's arm around my back.

I let him lift me without any help because my head felt as though it might fall from my neck if I didn't keep a tight hold on it, and I wasn't sure if it was from the fight I'd had with a ghost in the mirror or the vision Delilah had given me. I needed to be alone, but from the looks on the faces surrounding my bed, that didn't seem to be happening any time soon. I pushed the vision away so that I could deal with the present problem of the four people gathered in my room.

Mom sat beside me, and Dad stood with his hand on my shoulder. Jake had stepped away and promptly jammed his hands in his pockets while Rachel slipped both of her hands around his right forearm.

"What happened?" Mom dabbed my face with the rag again.

I pushed away the rag and scooted from beneath my dad's hand despite the immediate, sharp pain the movement caused in my head. I didn't want anyone *or anything* to touch me. I had no explanation that she would understand and none that I wanted to give. I couldn't tell her the truth, and I didn't want to. I was ashamed I'd let things get to this point.

"Miriam, you will tell me what happened—now." This time my mother's tone was less gentle.

I touched the spot high on my forehead where my hairline met the skin of my face. Other than a quarter-size knot, I didn't feel any other damage. Had I hit just a half-inch lower, I probably would have split the skin. My hair must have cushioned the blow. Glancing between Mom and Dad, I looked at the shattered mirror. I could see a cardboard backing where the glass was completely gone at the top of the mirror. The bottom, though webbed with cracks was still inside the wooden frame.

I couldn't meet her eyes. I tried to stay as close to the truth as possible. "I was sick to my stomach, and I threw up." I pointed to my bathroom where I wasn't even sure I'd flushed earlier. "I got light-headed, and, I guess, I tripped and fell." I pointed in the general direction of the mirror and hoped there was actually something on the floor to make the excuse of tripping logical.

I could feel Jake's skepticism without looking in his direction. He'd heard the commotion. He'd heard me fighting with the mist coming from the mirror. He knew I wasn't being completely honest.

"This has gone on long enough. You have to go to the doctor." Mom stood as she spoke and looked at Dad.

"And tell him what? I tripped and hit my head?" I knew I sounded surly and mean, and I closed my eyes again to get control of my temper. I couldn't let her take me to the doctor. I had gotten myself into this, and I had to find a way out myself. My shame at the mess I'd made wouldn't allow her to help me, and I wasn't just talking about the glass shards scattered on the floor. I was in control of my own body, or at least I used to be, and I had to fix this. If I didn't, I was afraid I'd never have control again.

With a churning stomach, I realized I should never have listened to the voice, should never have chased after this thing. I didn't have proof that any of it was real. I wasn't even sure I believed it myself. I'd just had my head slammed into a mirror. I might not be able to prove Delilah existed, but the pain in my head was very real—and very scary.

I looked up at my father, his green eyes meeting mine. He ran a hand through his chestnut curls, then pushed up his glasses before putting his hands on his hips. "You stay home tomorrow and do absolutely nothing, understood?"

A day out of school should sound heavenly, but the work that I knew I'd be missing already felt like a weight around my shoulders, but if staying home would appease my parents and keep me out of the doctor's office, that's exactly what I'd do. I nodded.

Mom huffed and glared at Dad. "She hasn't been sleeping, and she complains of a headache continuously. She skipped class today, and she could have been seriously hurt tonight. Do you really think a day home wi—"

"You asked my opinion, Rebekah," he said, holding his hands up in surrender and shaking his head.

"Technically, I didn't." She tossed the rag at his chest and mumbled something about men under her breath as she turned for the door, stopping just before she stepped into the hall. "Fine. You win this time, Miriam, but I'd better see a drastic improvement, or I'm making an appointment."

My dad bent and kissed the top of my head. "Love you, kiddo. I'll check on you later."

I nodded, and he left. Then I turned to meet the accusation on Jake's face. He'd barely spoken to me in days, but I remembered the look of concern he'd given me before I'd rushed up to my room earlier. He'd nearly broken the door to try to get to me, and for that I was grateful. I wasn't sure what would have happened if he hadn't come in. I was afraid the vision wouldn't have been all she would have done if he hadn't interrupted.

He narrowed his eyes as he came around the end of my bed. Rachel moved to the glass shards on the floor. Reaching for the small trash can I kept near my desk, she wordlessly began to pick up the pieces and drop them in the can. Jake looked from the mirror back to me.

"That's a load of BS. You didn't trip and fall. I heard you. That wasn't the sound of a fall." His gray eyes searched my face for the truth. "Something isn't right. Things have been weird with you for weeks. You can keep sayin' it's stress or whatever, but I don't believe you. You can't keep it hidden forever." His accusation hit me hard. The lines on his forehead and the dip in his brow told me he loved me regardless if he said it or not. He held my eyes for a minute longer before turning for the door.

Rachel continued to pick up the glass until the can was full then, can in hand, she sat on the side of my bed and just stared at me for a minute until I began to squirm a little under the scrutiny. She could read me even better than Mom. Frowning, she said, "I'll bring your work home tomorrow and help you get caught up." She softly gripped my forearm with her free hand. "And you can tell me what's really happening. You'll be ready by then. I'll listen, and we *will* figure out what to do." It wasn't a request.

Pushing down the quick anger that had been my companion all day, I nodded as she stood with the can. I would tell her. And she would help. I pretended that I didn't have a choice while relief washed over me. As she left, she started to pull the door closed behind her, and I sat up quickly, causing dizziness and swift pain to rush to my head.

"No, leave it open please," I said. She nodded and walked away. I promised myself I wouldn't be alone with Delilah again, knowing all the while I could never outrun my own mind.

CHAPTER 32

I'd been rolling my latest vision of Delilah around in my head all day. Phoebe Tadmor, Nurse Tadmor, was the girl in the vision. My teacher and Jake's coach, our principal, and now the school nurse had all tormented Delilah Ezra. When I thought back to the boiler scene I'd experienced a couple of days ago, I remembered the same blonde hair and the boys calling her by name. She'd been in both visions; the high-pitched laughter when they'd been playing their sick game of hide-and-seek had been hers.

Before the visions, I hadn't realized the three had attended Thomasville High, but the fact that they all attended the same school, my school, was the least far-fetched part of this story, and while I might be surprised by Coach Joseph and Mr. Shiloh's behavior, I could definitely see the nurse in the role of tormentor.

How would I feel if some mean girl told me to kill myself? Would it drive me to suicide? I doubted it, but then I never imagined I'd be seeing a spirit girl's life in my head, that I'd want to bash in the head of my best friend, or that I'd be worried about failing tests. I also wasn't Delilah. I didn't know exactly how she'd felt despite seeing some of her memories, and I still didn't know how she died.

I Googled Delilah Ezra but only had hits of current Delilah's, women who were still alive and had Facebook, Twitter, and Instagram accounts. She probably had an obituary, but I'd likely have to dig through physical copies or microfilm, something else I had to Google when I searched 'finding 80s obituaries.'

I was pretty certain the high school library kept copies of old yearbooks, so I texted Rachel around noon when I knew she'd secretly check her phone at lunch and asked her to bring home yearbooks from 11985, 986, 1987, and 1988. Philip graduated in '86 according to the photos in the stadium lobby. Dee had to be around the same age since she was in high school at the same time. Maybe they were like Jake and me, separated by a year or less. I told Rachel that I'd explain it all when she brought my homework to me that afternoon, and I meant it.

After reliving Delilah's horror with the popular girls, I realized how much I needed and wanted Rachel's friendship back. I couldn't go through this alone. As close as I normally was with my mother, I just didn't feel like she was the person to confide in. She and Dad might love all things antique and the stories that come along with those items, but they would draw the line at a ghost attaching itself to one of those things. They were both too logical for that. They'd attribute it to stress again and likely get me a therapist, which would be the least helpful thing ever.

I slid the clover along the chain in a gesture that was beginning to feel normal as I waited for Rachel's reply. I didn't know how I'd ever explain the weird mixed emotions I was having about helping Delilah. I couldn't shake the need to help her even though the idea of it scared me beyond belief. But every time I thought about letting it all go, something screamed inside of me, and I wasn't sure if it was me or her.

How could I even consider helping Delilah? She'd scared the life out of me more than once. She'd attacked me through the mirror and had me questioning my sanity. Assuming I wasn't just losing my mind and Delilah's ghost was really communicating, I didn't have a clue what she even wanted. So, how could I consider helping? Because every time she scared me, she showed me something horrible that happened to her, something that made me hate her persecutors and want what? Revenge?

If I managed to rip the necklace from my neck, would Delilah release me? Would she disappear if I destroyed the necklace? I touched the bump that remained in my hairline and cringed slightly at the soreness. I doubted anything but doing whatever she wanted would stop her now. The necklace might have been the conduit or the catalyst for connecting with me, but if she had truly somehow taken control of Ruth Claudia, she'd done so without the necklace. It had been safely inside the glass case when Ruth had grabbed my arm and led me to the dining room.

Even today with no one in the house but me, the anger remained simmering, like a covered pot threatening to boil over. And if I let the feelings go, like that pot, I'd have a terrible mess. I had no choice. To get Delilah out of my life, I'd have "free" her—whatever that meant. But I needed to know what happened to her in the first place before I could begin to fix it.

My phone buzzed. Rachel sent a thumbs up emoji, so I knew she would bring the yearbooks. I allowed myself a moment's relief. Rachel was the smartest girl I knew. She and I would unravel this mystery together.

CHAPTER 33

"You should have told me all this when you first suspected." Rachel, her bulging bag between us on the bed, shook her head. "You must have been terrified."

"I was more angry than anything." Even as I said it, I felt my unwanted companion seething inside me, whispering about Rachel's selfishness, telling me she was only there because she wanted to look good in front of Jake, but I pushed the voice and the feeling down. As soon as Rachel walked into my room, the story tumbled out like a waterfall. I'd told her about meeting Ruth Claudia, how she didn't remember buying the necklace, the vision of Delilah in the kitchen, the mist holding me to the mirror, the dreamscapes where I'd seen and felt Delilah's torment—everything. Rachel wanted to help because she cared about me and because she'd been my only friend for longer than anyone else in my sixteen years. She listened, her mouth gaping at times, and had hardly spoken.

I flipped open the top of her backpack. "I just hope this helps."

"It will, or if it doesn't, we'll look somewhere else. There's an answer somewhere, and we are exactly the girls to find it." She smiled and dragged a yearbook emblazoned with a neon-green 'T' on the front. The messy scribbled lettering read, "Thomasville High School 1986" in neon pink and "Our Future's So Bright" in neon yellow—a tribute to the 80s for sure.

"What's the guy's name again?" She flipped open the first page.

"Philip Ezra," I said, taking the 1985 yearbook from her bag. I needed a timeline, a way of tracing Dee and her brother, but more than that, I wanted some kind of confirmation, something to show I wasn't totally insane.

"Here he is!" Rachel held the book closer to her face for a better view. "Whoa, he's cute! Take away that feathery hair, and he'd be super-hot." She turned the book around to face me, and sure enough, there was the photo I'd seen in the stadium hallway, only a little larger. Though the page was black and white, his eyes remained engaging.

I grabbed my phone from my bedside table and easily found the photo I snapped the night I'd run into Dee and ditched Rachel. We put the two photos together though it was really pointless since they were obviously the same guy.

"I take that back. In color, I can totally forgive the feathered hair. Those eyes!" Rachel leaned closer to my phone.

"I know." I shivered. "Those eyes have been in my dreams, in my head, in my dumb mirror! He and Delilah have the same eyes."

"Well, that's definitely him." She held her place with one finger and flipped the pages backward. "You said you think she's his little sister?"

I nodded. "But not little, little. Maybe a year or two? Coach and Mr. Shiloh were around Philip's age, so I'm assuming she was, too."

Rachel shook her head but didn't look up from the pages as she scanned the names along the margin. "That's so weird and just—" she cringed "—gross. Coach Joseph and Mr. Shiloh as teenage bullies? Ew."

"You should've seen it." The memory of their leering faces flashed into my head. "They weren't only bullies, Rach. Coach at least was borderline rapist." I opened the '85 yearbook and found the section marked "Juniors." Reason dictated that Philip had to have been a junior that year, so I'd start there.

"She's not a freshman." Rachel turned another page and began scanning the sophomore class list. "Now, Nurse Tadmor, I could definitely see her as a bully." I found Philip in the juniors and turned back a year, just as Rachel thumped her finger hard on the page she had open. "I got her! Delilah Ezra, class of 1987."

She turned the book toward me, and sure enough, there was a dark-haired, unsmiling girl on the second row from the top. The same heavily-fringed eyes stared back, and goosebumps broke out along my arms. I'd never seen Delilah in my dreams; I'd *been* her. But Dee? I'd spoken to her, had coffee with her for goodness sake.

Dee had been fairy pretty, like a perfect pixie. Delilah, not so much. Her hair seemed the same color, but the photo was black and white, so it was impossible to tell if it was black or dark brown. The style screamed 80s perm, big and kinky, and definitely longer than Dee's. Her features lacked the symmetry of Philip's. Lips almost too full, nose a little turned up at the end. Dee's face had made me think of a model or at least the star of some teen show. Was this the same face? In that moment, it was hard to tell.

"Is this Dee?" Rachel asked the very question rolling in my brain. And honestly, I wasn't sure.

"My gut says 'yes,' but I'm not sure." I held the page closer as though proximity might turn on the switch of certainty. "She had short dark hair but more whimsical, ya know?" Rachel's raised brow told me she didn't know. "Like cutesy, curling around her ears. This girl's hair is frizzy, and Dee's face was pretty, one of those girls you and I usually pick apart because we're jealous." I slid the clover along its chain.

Rachel snorted and turned the book back in her direction. "Yeah, we'd be more 'bless her heart' with this one."

"See if you can find her anywhere else in there. I'll keep looking in this one."

An hour later, we'd made only a small dent in our mystery. We knew Delilah hadn't graduated in 1987 as expected or at least not from Thomasville High School since she wasn't pictured with the graduating class. She hadn't been involved in anything in 1985 or 1986, not cheer or band or any clubs. Philip was all over the place—president of this club, vp of another, football player, Most Likely to Succeed, and Mr. THS. People loved Philip, and that must have left poor Delilah feeling pretty left out. Pity for her left me feeling unsettled and doubting that Delilah and Dee could possibly be the same person.

"Maybe it's a Dr. Jekyll thing," Rachel said as she opened the can of cola she'd retrieved from the kitchen. "Delilah is this plain, almost-ugly girl with a hot, popular brother, and when she died—" Rachel's mouth turned down at one corner as she whispered the last word "—she transformed into Dee, became what she wasn't in life." She shrugged. "Makes as much sense as any of the rest of this."

I opened my cola. "They're so different but so similar somehow. The dark hair, the eyes, the jewelry. Dream Philip said Delilah liked gold jewelry, and every time I've seen her she's been wearing it. And she was so worried about ruining her dress when she'd been hiding in the boiler room. Dee is always dressed to the nines, like she just stepped out of a magazine. It has to be her, right?"

"I'm following your lead on this one." She scooted closer to me where I leaned against the headboard and nudged me with her shoulder. "After all, you're the cra-cra one who's seeing stuff." I cut my eyes toward her, and she grinned. "You know I'm kidding. And yes, I think Delilah and Dee are the same person. They have to be."

"But we still don't know much more than we did." I thumbed the edges of the yearbook I held in my hands without really seeing the pages.

"We need to talk to somebody who knew the Ezra family." Rachel took a sip of soda, but a drop landed on her baby-blue chiffon top. As I reached for the paper towel I used as a makeshift coaster on my table, another image leapt into my mind. I quickly flipped through the yearbook I held as Rachel whined and brushed at the spot. I finally landed on the "Faculty and Staff" page and ran a finger down the names listed across to the photo of a much younger woman than the one who'd dropped coffee on the table days ago. Ruth Claudia.

"This is it, Rach. This is our link to the past."

CHAPTER 34

"Let's search Delilah's brother before we try to find Ruth."
Rachel shrugged one shoulder. "Maybe we'll get lucky and find
a social media account."

I wasn't sure what we'd say even if we did. "Hey, could your
sister be an avenging spirit who's haunting me" just didn't
sound quite appropriate. As it turns out, I needn't have worried
about what to say anyway. Googling "Philip Ezra" just showed
us NOT to Google "Philip Ezra."

Rachel ran her finger down the mousepad and the name
slipped by attached to various links. "There are over five
thousand results! How is that possible? Should we start with
the sex offenders or the census hits on descendents.com?" She
shook her head but smiled suddenly and turned to look from
the screen to me. "Let's try an image search. He'd be a lot older,
but maybe we'll recognize those baby blues." Turning back to
the screen, she clicked the image search option, but that didn't
help. She scrolled down for several minutes before pointing to
the screen. "This is crazy. Look. That's not even a guy."

Sure enough, a pretty redhead in a pristine white gown
trailed her hand along the top of almost waist high grass
and wildflowers. The bottom right corner of the image was
embossed with "P. Ezra Photography."

"Great." I sank back against my headboard. "There's a
photographer with that name. Any search will pull up every
photograph he's posted." I rubbed my eyes with the heels of my
palms. I needed to get to the bottom of all of this. I needed to
know why Delilah Ezra had chosen me and what she wanted
from me. I'd have to wait for Dee to show me those answers, or

I'd have to find them out from someone who knew her.

Rachel scooted up beside me, bringing the laptop with her. She nudged me with her shoulder again till I gave her a weary glance. "We'll find help. I promise." Her diamond stud earrings sparkled in the lamplight from my side table as she tucked her dark hair behind her ear. She looked so hopeful, so sure, that I felt I'd be letting her down if I voiced my doubts. So I only nodded and reached for the open yearbook still on the bed. I ran my finger over Philip's photograph.

Instinctively, I reached for the pendant. If I could trust Delilah's visions, Philip had given her this pendant because he loved her, not as a birthday gift or Christmas present but just because. I almost felt as much of an obligation to Philip now as I did to Delilah. Her spirit couldn't rest, and if I could help her, some part of me felt I should.

I looked back at Rachel. "Should we switch gears and look for Ruth Claudia instead? Maybe she could give us *something*, and she's local. At least, I think she is—unless she's been a figment of my imagination all along, in which case—" I tried to smile and sound like I was only joking "—just don't tell me, or I'm going to cover my head with this blanket and never leave the room." I made the joke to cover how scared I really was. Every day, I felt like I was losing myself to this obsession. I wanted free just like Delilah, but I had no idea how to do that.

Rachel wasn't fooled. She dropped her arm around my shoulders and squeezed me to her side for a minute before releasing me and putting her hands back on the keyboard.

"Alright, new search." Rachel typed the retired teacher's name into the search bar, and like Philip's search (but with fewer pervy-looking guys) the results continued for several pages, but unlike Philip, the top result showed a local address. Rachel grabbed my phone from the bedside table. "Screenshot it," she said, motioning to the laptop.

After I clicked the camera button, I touched the thumbnail of the shot to make sure I'd captured the address clearly. "What'll we say if we find her?" I looked back at Rachel.

Sighing, she picked up the yearbook, flipping back to Delilah's photo. "When we find her, not 'if.' When we find her, we'll tell her it's for a project, which isn't exactly a lie. We'll say our history class is working on a social experiment, finding out about some of our past graduates and where they are now. But I think we should ask about Philip, not Delilah. We can work our way up to her, ask about his family and stuff. Might scare her if we start off talking about a dead girl. I think it's safe to say Delilah's story didn't end on a positive note."

I absently rubbed the pendant between my thumb and index finger. "Yeah, you're probably right." When I glanced back at Rachel, she was watching me so intently that I dropped the pendant back to my chest and quickly busied myself with closing the laptop and gathering the yearbooks.

"She killed herself, huh?" Rachel's question made me stop and look at her. Her caramel eyes were sad, and I wondered if she was beginning to feel as connected to Delilah as I was. "Delilah committed suicide."

This time it wasn't a question but a statement we both knew intuitively had to be true. I nodded. "Yeah, I think so."

"That's why she wants you to free her. She's trapped here with unfinished business. Isn't that what they always say on those paranormal, ghosty shows?"

I slid the yearbooks onto my table and laid my laptop and phone on top of them. "I guess. You've watched more of those things than I have," I teased, knowing how much she complained about her grandmother's choice of television programs.

"Only 'cause Gram likes them." She shivered. "Never thought I'd be stuck in an episode, though." Rachel's face brightened, and she sat up straighter. "Hey! We should talk to my gram! She might be able to help us."

It wasn't a terrible idea. Esther might be a little eccentric with her ever-present sparkles and flashy clothes, but she'd always been nice to me, and she did watch every supernatural show on TV. But I wasn't exactly sure how she'd take the news that her granddaughter's best friend was being haunted by a possibly malevolent, definitely horrifying teenage spirit.

"That's not a bad idea." I didn't want to discount what might turn out to be a brilliant suggestion. "But I want to try to figure it out on my own first, okay?"

Rachel smiled but shook her head, putting her hand on top of mine. "You mean we're going to try to figure it out."

I smiled till my eyes found my broken mirror across the room. I couldn't—wouldn't—let Rachel get hurt.

CHAPTER 35

"I think this is it." The single-story house in front of me looked postcard perfect. With its light-blue paint and huge maple trees blazing their fall colors, it seemed like the kind of house you'd see on a realtor's ad with a happy, young couple kissing behind the 'sold' sign. Even the cream and yellow mums sitting on either side of the white-railed porch seemed staged in their flawlessness. Ruth Claudia definitely had a great setup.

"Hope she's home," Rachel said from beside me. We'd borrowed Grandma Esther's Nissan rather than have Jake bring us to avoid any questions we didn't want to answer. "Maybe we should've called."

"Yeah, maybe." I glanced at my watch. It was about a quarter till six. We'd waited a few days to make this trip, partly because I'd put it off. I wanted to know the truth, but I wasn't looking forward to lying to the sweet old lady.

I'd also begun to doubt myself again.

Nothing had happened since I'd slammed my head against my mirror, and my rational brain was beginning to think I'd made the whole thing up. The sore spot near my hairline would argue otherwise, but things had been so normal since I'd spilled the beans to Rachel. Ordinary even. I hadn't had a vision or a nightmare or heard a voice since that night, and the part of me that had always prized control argued that I'd tripped and fallen into the mirror. I'd been so stressed lately maybe I'd made it all up. I ran the clover along the chain, wondering if turning around and leaving might not be better. It felt stupid and wrong to be standing here debating on talking to some retired teacher about a suicidal teenager she may or may not remember. I wasn't comfortable pumping her for information nor was I happy about the partial truth we'd be telling her to get into her house. A partial truth was really just a whole lie when you got down to it and was wrong anyway you tried to justify it.

"Maybe we shou—"

"Uh-uh, no way. We are not leaving. We're doing this." She tapped my forehead lightly with her index finger. "I know what's going on in that head of yours. I can practically see the wheels spinning. You're thinking about leaving." She grabbed my hand. "Nope, not happening. If you don't want to do the talking, I will, but we are going in that house if she's home."

She pulled me along a few steps up the walk until she was certain I was following, but she glanced over her shoulder anyway before pulling open the screen door. Mrs. Claudia had a glass and screen storm door, the kind that could be opened to let in air in good weather, and I cringed a little when Rachel knocked boldly on the white wooden door behind the storm door. This was it. No turning back now.

I tugged nervously at the strap on my messenger bag. I'd brought a notebook to add legitimacy to our 'assignment' excuse that we'd worked on in advance but also to jot down notes for real to mull over later.

The door swung open after a minute or so, and Ruth Claudia appeared. She was wearing what Mom calls a muumuu, a loose, shapeless gown meant to cover but not really flatter. Its orange and white hibiscus flowers practically screamed from the teal background. Her short, white hair was pushed back from her face with a severe headband, combs gripping the hair with tiny plastic teeth. Her cheeks were rosy without makeup, and she was wearing tortoiseshell glasses that were a shade darker than the suede slippers on her feet. She was adorable in a grandma kind of way.

She smiled and said, "What can I do for you girls? Selling something for school?"

Rachel stepped to the side as far as the screen door would allow so that I could be front and center. She gave me a "go-get-'em" little push, and I smiled in what I hoped was a disarming way. "Do you remember me, Ms. Claudia? We met a little while back at the coffee shop not far from the school."

She cocked her head, and her brows drew together like she was concentrating on my face, then she smiled. "Oh yes, I remember you! The necklace, right? But I'm afraid you'll have to refresh me on your name."

"Ria. Yes, we talked about my necklace. This is Rachel." I motioned to Rachel without looking at her, and she stretched out her hand, which Ms. Claudia shook.

"Nice to meet you, ma'am." Rachel seemed to know how difficult the lie was for me because she quickly added, "We have a school project we wanted to ask you about if you have a minute."

"Me?" Ruth put her hand to her chest, and I noticed the two silver bracelets and chunky silver ring she was wearing, despite the fact that she was clearly having an afternoon at home.

"Yes, ma'am. Ria mentioned meeting you, and when we were assigned research on a former graduate, we both thought you might give us some information since we're having trouble finding out a lot about him." Rachel moved ahead of me once again, tucking her glossy dark locks behind her ear and reaching for Ruth's hand. She gasped in an exaggerated manner. "OOO, I love your bracelet."

Ms. Claudia stretched out her arm to give Rachel a better view. "Do you? I just got it in the mail today. I ordered it from one of those home shopping channels—got it for a steal because it was on clearance!" She touched Rachel's fingers, which rested gently on her arm. "Why don't you two come inside? I'll get us some tea, and we'll have a nice visit."

When Ruth turned to lead us inside, Rachel wiggled her brows at me and smiled mischievously. "Never make fun of my jewelry obsession again."

I had to smile as I shook my head and motioned for her to follow the old lady. "Jewelry, breaking borders across generations."

"Yeah, I'd say so." She flicked the clover pendant before walking inside as Ruth disappeared into what I assumed was the kitchen.

My stomach clenched. If I could trust my senses, then I really had crossed not only generations but also spiritual realms with this necklace. It connected me to a dead girl and her brother. I'd spoken a strange truth without realizing it.

We stepped into the foyer and let the door close behind us. Ruth stuck her head out around the doorway. I could see a counter and white and blue tile behind her. "Please sit." She motioned toward a room to our left where an overstuffed lavender couch sat. "I'll just get our drinks and be right out. Make yourselves at home." She smiled before ducking back into the kitchen.

Rachel shrugged one shoulder and started across the pine floor. We sat on the couch, and I could feel my feet sink into the plush gray rug before us. Rachel pulled a blue legal pad and pen from her backpack and motioned that I should get out my notebook, too, to keep our story legit. I mouthed, "Oh yeah," and she gave a little eye roll, mouthing back, "Relax."

Ruth came back in carrying a wicker tray with three glasses of iced tea, each with a lemon slice split and garnishing the rim of the glass. On a small blue and white toile plate was half a dozen chocolate chip cookies.

"I baked these fresh today. I don't know why I do that. Goodness knows I don't need any cookies!" She set the tray on the low whitewashed coffee table in front of the couch. She handed both us a glass. "I like my tea sweet, a lot of sugar and a little tea, that's what my daughter always says." Ruth sat in the gray recliner across from the couch, sinking back with a sigh as though she'd been walking a mile instead of the ten steps from her kitchen. She quickly put out her hand toward me. "By the way, Ria, I spoke to my doctor about my not being able to remember buying your necklace." She gestured toward the pendant. "He did a complete work-up and didn't find a thing wrong, which might be even scarier than if he had!" She shook her head. "Guess it was just a crazy old lady thing." She chuckled. "Now then, tell me about this assignment." She pulled her lemon slice from the rim of her tea and plopped it in before taking a sip and setting it on the table beside her chair. An open romance novel rested pages down on the table, so I assumed that was her usual spot.

After a quick side glance at me, Rachel began, "Well, we were given an old yearbook and asked to pick a senior from that year's graduating class. Then we were supposed to research this person, where are they now kind of thing. It's part of a sociology unit we're doing this nine weeks." The lie slipped so smoothly from her mouth that I began to wonder if Rachel had ever lied to me. Judging from her ability, I doubt I would have known it. I made a mental note to ask her later why she was such a proficient liar.

"I see," Ms. Claudia said. "Who did you pick?"

"Philip Ezra, senior 1986. Do you remember him?" Rachel asked, clicking her pen and turning to a new page in her legal pad.

Ruth frowned. "Did you say Philip Ezra?"

Rachel nodded, and I pulled the yearbook from my bag, finally finding my voice. "We have the yearbook if you need to see him to help you remember."

I flipped to the sticky note we'd put in the other day when

we found his photo. I started to hand her the book, but she shook her head.

"No need. I remember that young man quite clearly." She scooted conspiratorially forward to the edge of the recliner as though to share a secret. "You two chose him out of all those seniors?" She motioned toward the book where it rested in my lap, and my stomach flip-flopped again. I licked my suddenly dry lips.

Rachel nodded. "Yes, ma'am. Why? Is he a bad choice? We've had some trouble finding him online. That's one reason we came to you, to see if you can point us to where he might be now."

Ms. Claudia shook her head. "I'm afraid you might need to choose someone else. I can tell you exactly where he is. He's dead."

CHAPTER 36

I'd never really understood that saying about being knocked over with a feather until that moment. I blinked rapidly and shook my head. "Did you say he died?" I couldn't possibly have heard correctly. Philip Ezra was dead.

She nodded, then closed her eyes for a moment as she shook her head. "Such a tragedy! Shakespearean if you will. That poor family. Neither of you have heard this story?" She didn't wait for us to answer, and it was clear this was a woman who'd spent her adult life telling stories to classrooms of students. Eyes large, she paused for only a moment before saying, "Well, I suppose you wouldn't know about it. You're just babies, and it was thirty years ago. Philip died mysteriously a year—" she looked up as though searching for the correct year on the ceiling of her living room "—two years after he graduated. He'd moved off to go to college somewhere up north, Yale or Princeton, somewhere Ivy League. He was so smart. I tell you, he was one of the brightest kids I ever had *and* attractive to boot. He had the run of that school." She shook her head and took a drink of tea.

Rachel and I looked at each other during her dramatic pause before she finally began again.

"Anyway, where was I? Oh, run of the school." She waved her hand as though dismissing something we'd said, even though neither of us had spoken. "He went off to some expensive, fancy school. Most people thought his grandfather, Jonathan, got him in by pulling some strings, but I don't believe that. I'm certain he earned his way, too smart to be otherwise. He met some girl while he was there." She dropped her voice to a whisper and put up her hand as though to shield her mouth from strangers overhearing. "Got her in the family way apparently because after he died she showed up with a baby, and last I heard, Philip's parents had adopted her."

Angel. She had to be talking about the pretty, well-dressed woman I'd spoken to the day of the estate sale. She was the illegitimate daughter of Philip Ezra.

"Such a shame." Ruth stared across the room for a moment.

"You said he died mysteriously. What did you mean?" Rachel's voice actually made me jump a little because I was so lost in the story and my own thoughts.

Ruth swung her eyes back to us excitedly. "Oh yes! Sorry, I get side-tracked these days." She chuckled. "Yes, his death was all hush-hush, but from what I heard, it was suicide, which is even more tragic because his younger sister committed suicide the year before."

Philip had committed suicide? Delilah's confidante, her protector, had killed himself a year after his sister? It had to be connected.

"His sister, what was her name? It was something weird, something uncommon." Ruth snapped her fingers. "Delilah! That's it. But Philip always called her Dee."

At the mention of her name, my stomach completely dropped, and I had to tighten my grip on my paper and pen to stop the slight tremor there. It was confirmation I hadn't needed. Delilah and Dee were the same person.

Rachel's hand discreetly touched the side of my thigh almost in a reassuring way, as though to remind me she was with me and not to freak out. "Why would he kill himself?" she asked.

Ruth paused mid-drink and swallowed quickly. "Who knows? But I heard he went nuts. You know, that sometimes happens when kids go away to school. Maybe the stress was too much, or maybe he didn't want to marry that girl." She shrugged. "You just never know."

Or maybe his dead sister started showing up in his mirror, begging for his help.

I took a deep breath and asked what I really needed to know. "So why did his sister kill herself?"

If Ruth thought it was strange for me to ask about Delilah, she didn't show it. She set her tea back on the table and reached across for a cookie before sinking back into her chair. I guess Delilah's story wasn't edge-of-your-seat interesting.

"Well, I didn't actually have her in class, but according to the gossip in the teacher's lounge, she couldn't handle her brother being gone."

"She killed herself because Philip went away to college?" I asked.

"I don't know, dear, that's just what I heard, but she was always a sad little thing. Sad in a pitiful sort of way and not near as popular as Philip was. If I'm remembering right, she wasn't as attractive as him. Her whole family lived up in that big ol' house, and I guess she was so wrapped up in her brother that she couldn't handle being the only young person there. My partner teacher, Mary, who taught next door had Delilah in class, and she used to try to talk to her, but Delilah never really warmed up to her, to anyone from what Mary said. Mary always said it was a shame Philip was so much prettier than Delilah."

"Wow, I'm impressed with how much you remember, Ms. Claudia." Rachel reached for a cookie as well, and I wasn't sure if was because she really wanted one or because she was ingratiating herself to Ruth as she'd done with the bracelet earlier to keep her talking. But I doubted Ruth Claudia needed a reason to keep talking. She seemed more than happy to spill everything she could remember about the Ezra kids.

"Well, you don't soon forget a brother and sister suicide, hon. In fact, I'd say it strengthens what memories you have."

"Was Delilah bullied after Philip left? That's the leading cause of suicide in teenagers." I added the last part when I realized the question might seem a little random, not knowing if it were true or not.

"Bullied? Not that I'm aware of. I'd say most kids steered clear of her before and after he left. Have you ever seen those old cartoons where the little dog follows the big bulldog around, goes around and around him in circles, trying his hardest to get noticed? That little dog was kind of like Delilah. I always saw her on the fringe of Philip and his friends. He didn't ignore her, but he didn't seem to try to drag her into the group either."

Delilah wasn't bullied? That didn't fit with any of the visions she'd shown me. But teachers don't notice everything. Maybe Ruth had just never seen the bullying; after all, she had never had Delilah in class. "So you never saw anyone pick on her? Did you ever see Philip have to defend her?"

Ruth looked across the room again, presumably searching her memory, and Rachel took the opportunity to give me another big-eyed look like she was trying to tell me I was being too pushy with my questions.

Ruth turned back, her mouth a flat line as she shook her head again. "No, hon, I never saw that, never heard anyone mention that to my recollection. Seemed like most people just ignored her."

I knew I was open-mouthed, staring in shock. People ignored Delilah? She wasn't bullied? If she wasn't bullied, what pushed her to suicide? What did that say about the visions she'd shown me? Did that mean all of those images had been fake?

Rachel took a quick drink to wash down the cookie, then stood and motioned for me to follow. "Ms. Claudia, we really appreciate this. We'll let our teacher know that we should probably switch people."

I nodded. "Thank you for all of your help." I put my notebook and the yearbook back into my bag while Rachel did the same.

"By the way, who is your teacher?" She hauled herself jerkily to her feet. "Curiosity." She winked.

"Coach Joseph," I answered without thinking.

"Bart Joseph? I didn't realize he was teaching at Thomasville! Such a sweet boy. He was one of Philip's friends. Ran him out of my room so I could start class more times than I could count. He and that other kid ...what was his name?" She tapped her front tooth with her fingernail. "Paul! Paul, yes, they were just about inseparable."

Rachel turned so quickly that her backpack slammed against my arm. "Paul Shiloh?"

"Yes, last I heard he was an assistant principal in the middle school." Ruth put her hands backward on her hips and smiled broadly.

I gulped, like a real gulp. "He's our principal now." Dang. I probably should've seen that coming. She knows my teacher *and* my principal. I hoped she wouldn't see either of them anytime soon.

"Is that right?" She made her way to the door in front of us. Rachel yanked on my bag strap, but I didn't turn around. Instead, I followed Ruth to the door.

When we reached the door that she'd opened by now, I gave her what I hoped was a believable smile. "Thanks again, Ms. Claudia."

"Good luck," she said with a pat to my back. For a second, I thought she was talking about my problem with Delilah. The surprise must have shown in my face because she quickly added, "With your project. I hope you get someone with a much brighter story next time."

181

I nodded and vaguely heard Rachel thank Ruth as I stepped out onto the walkway. I'd come here hoping to find a link to Philip, validation of Delilah's story. The reality, according to Ruth Claudia, was vastly different. A dull ache had set up shop behind my eyes, and I realized I'd been gritting my teeth so hard I'd given it to myself. I grabbed the necklace and gave it a hard tug, all the while knowing it wouldn't do any good. I needed to think. I needed to be alone.

I turned as Rachel came down the walk. She started to speak, but I shook my head, tears filling my eyes. "I can't. I just—"

Rachel nodded. "I get it. Do you want a ride home?"

I shook my head and turned from her. I made it a few steps before the tears came, and then I ran. I ran blindly down the sidewalk, not really caring where I was going. I knew it was stupid. I knew it wouldn't help, but I ran anyway. The funny thing is you can't outrun yourself.

CHAPTER 37

"It's not a coincidence, the age difference." Rachel sounded so certain that it wasn't hard to picture the stern set of her mouth and the matter-of-fact look in her eyes. We'd been on the phone for at least a half an hour by now, rehashing all Ruth had told us. "You and Jake, Delilah and Philip, the age difference has to be close. Maybe that's why she chose you." She didn't have to add that the difference in popularity was close, too.

Philip may not have been a football star like Jake, but I'll bet Jake and Philip both shared the limelight in a similar way. Rachel was too sweet to say it out loud, but she had to have seen that as well as I did. Delilah and I both had popular brothers who were a year or so older than us. I hoped I wasn't the pathetic follower that Ruth Claudia made Delilah out to be, but in other kids' eyes, maybe I was. After all, I never really went anywhere unless it was an after-school study group or with my parents antiques shopping. Rachel had to drag me to that football game weeks ago and then I had bailed on her to spend the evening with a spirit girl who was trying to get me to do what I was starting believe was something bad, something wrong, to the people who had probably never even noticed her existence.

How had my life gotten so out of control?

My head throbbed. There had to be a solution somewhere amid all the questions, a way to satisfy Delilah so that she'd leave me alone while keeping my hands clean. I thought I'd seen the truth, thought she'd shown me the truth. I'd almost felt vindicated in getting back at Nurse Tadmor, Coach Joseph, and Mr. Shiloh. They'd been so horrible to Delilah, bullying in the extreme. She'd felt so helpless. I'd about convinced myself

I'd be justified in hurting them for hurting her, but now? After visiting Ruth, I wasn't sure any of what Delilah had shown me was true. And if I didn't do what Delilah wanted, how could I ever hope to be rid of her?

"You still there?" Rachel asked.

I nodded, even though she couldn't see me through the phone. "Yeah, I've got a headache, again."

"It's all related. You know it has to be. Dee, Delilah, whatever her name is, showed you that stuff to make her look like the victim when really she was just a wannabe who couldn't stand that she wasn't as popular as her brother—not that that's what you are!" She hastily added the last part although I wondered if that wasn't true as well.

Did I envy Jake's popularity? I definitely envied how everything seemed so simple for him. Friends, sports, the scholarship he was bound to be offered while I was consumed with good grades and impressive test scores. I couldn't deny it. I was a little jealous of Jake. Was that how Delilah had gotten me so easily? Had these feelings been her way inside my head?

I opened and closed my jaw in a vain effort to relieve the pain in my head. If I kept up this clenching, I was going to break a tooth. "I'm gonna get off the phone. I think I need to lie down."

"Okay, I'll talk to you tomorrow, and Ria, don't give up hope. I'm still with you. We *will* figure this out."

My eyes flooded again. I thought I'd cried myself out when I'd run home. Thankfully, no one had been home to ask me questions. Jake must have still been at practice, and Mom and Dad must have been at work.

"Thanks, friend." I didn't wait to hear her answer as I disconnected our call and tossed my phone on my bedside table. I showered when I got home, hoping to wash away the tears as well as the fatigue I seemed to carry all the time now.

I was tired of it all, tired of fighting something I could only see when it decided to show itself, tired of my head and body betraying me, tired of worrying about what to do (or not do). I wanted it over. I wanted everything to go back to normal. I wanted to feel normal again, and I closed my eyes wondering if Delilah had felt the same way before she killed herself.

****

I can't. I can't do it anymore. It'll be easier this way. Never to feel anything again, never to be hurt again. It'll be over quickly.

I tug on the length of rope hanging from the rafter. I glance around the attic. This is as good a place as any. At least this way, it won't be where others can see. My father and mother will find me and make sure it's not a spectacle. It'll be discreet and fast.

I climb down from the ladder-back chair I've pulled under the rope and wipe my dusty hands on my white nightgown. I catch my reflection in the large, oval mirror resting on the floor and leaning against the wall. I walk toward my reflection.

I wish it could be different. I wish so many things, but it's too late now. I've made up my mind, and I won't change it. My fingers brush the clover pendant hanging above the scoop neckline of my gown. Philip's gift. It makes me sad now to see it. He's gone. He's abandoned me like everyone else.

I reach up with both hands and unclasp the silver chain, dangling it before my face for a second as the opal catches the light from the single hanging bulb. I drop it into my palm and squeeze. I feel the prongs digging into my skin, and when I open my hand, I see tiny red bleeding welts from the stone. How appropriate. Philip has left me bleeding.

I hang the necklace over the top of the mirror, and the silver clinks once against the dirty glass. I walk back to the chair and step onto the seat, looping the rope around my neck. It's scratchy against my throat, but I pull on the knot to tighten it.

The pressure makes me panic for a moment, and a part of my brain screams 'NO!' but I can't stop. Before I can let myself chicken out, I kick the chair's back and hear it fall against the floor.

CHAPTER 38

My eyes flew open. I couldn't breathe. I tried to sit up, but something was holding me down. The force against my torso and hips felt like hands pushing. I flailed my legs and arms, but nothing helped. The more I struggled, the harder the force pushed. I opened my mouth to scream, but the necklace tightened around my throat.

I reached up to claw at the chain, but it grew tighter. I could feel the clover pressing against the hollow in my throat. I tried to pry the necklace loose enough to reach my finger under it, my nails scratching my skin, but I couldn't fit my finger between the necklace and my throat.

Dots danced in my vision before everything blurred. I was dying. Delilah was killing me for doubting her story, for not freeing her. She was killing me, and I would be with her forever. The thought brought a burst of adrenaline, and I thrashed my left arm against my bedside table, knocking my phone to the ground.

Not enough, not enough noise. I thrashed again, finding the table's edge and pushing with all of my strength to send the table and lamp crashing over.

Then I prayed. I prayed as I've never prayed before. I prayed with everything in me. I prayed to be released. I prayed for another breath. I prayed someone would hear the table falling.

I felt myself slipping under. Everything went black, and I wasn't sure if I'd closed my eyes or if my vision had finally failed. My struggles slowed. I tried to force my hands to work against the chain, but I didn't have the strength. My arms were so heavy, and they fell uselessly, one hanging over the bed's edge. This was it. This was the moment of my death.

Then I heard it. A voice outside my door. Jake. Jake was home. He called my name, but I couldn't speak, couldn't yell back. He pounded on the door. I vaguely realized he was slamming against it. It was jammed again, just like that first night I had the necklace when I heard my music box playing.

The door slammed against the wall, and Jake was there, grabbing me into his arms, patting my cheeks.

"Breathe, Ria!" I felt his hands at my throat, and suddenly the pressure there was gone.

My eyes flew open as I gulped air. I grabbed onto Jake's shirt as our eyes meet. His were panicked like I'd never seen them.

"What was that? What was happening?" His voice was loud, angry. "What's happening to you?"

I couldn't speak. My throat ached, and I reached up to feel for the necklace, but it was gone. I sat up quickly and spotted the chain and clover across the room where Jake must have thrown it. Jake had done it. He'd broken the chain. My brother had broken the necklace given to Delilah by her brother. I wrapped my arms around his shoulders and squeezed him to me hard, ignoring the spinning in my head.

"Thank you," I croaked with a scratchy voice.

But he wasn't satisfied. He pulled away, his face tense, his mouth an unyielding line. "Answer my question. What is happening to you?"

"Nothing. Not anymore because of you." Relief surged through me.

He pushed from the bed and looked down at me. "That's not an answer. I want the truth. You've been weird for weeks. Then you smashed your head against a mirror, and now—" he flipped his hand toward the necklace without looking at it "—a necklace is choking you to death! What the hell, Ria!"

"I want to tell you, Jake. I really do, but you won't believe it. I don't even believe it, and it's been happening to me!" My voice sounded like a sixty-year-old smoker.

He ran a hand through his curls and sighed heavily. "This have anything to do with wherever you and Rachel snuck off to do after school today?"

Rachel had told Jake she wouldn't be riding home with him, but she hadn't explained what we'd been doing. I nodded. "I ...I've..." I sighed. I was so tired, like bone tired. I couldn't explain it to him, not tonight. "I promise to tell you, but I can't tonight." I rubbed the spot around my throat. It stung and ached, and I knew when I woke up tomorrow, the mark would still be there. Something else to have to make up an excuse. I didn't try to stop the tears this time.

He sat back down beside me, dropping his arm around my shoulders the way he used to when we were little. "You'll tell me—soon, promise?"

I nodded, my eyes flooding with tears and my throat tightening for a different reason now. He started to get up, but I grabbed his forearm, pleading with my eyes. "Please stay for a few minutes. Please, Jake." I didn't want to be alone, and at that moment, I didn't care that I was being a total baby.

He sighed again but nodded as he propped his legs up on the bed, leaning back on the headboard and crossing his feet at the ankles. I clutched his arm to me and settled down on the pillows.

My heart still pounded, but gradually, I could feel calm returning, and I let my eyes slip closed. I was so tired.

****

When I opened my eyes, my room was dark. Where was Jake? I must have fallen asleep with him sitting next to me. My throat burned and ached, and a drink of water sounded heavenly.

Dropping my legs over the edge of the bed, I stood. I reached out to turn on my lamp before I remembered that it was smashed on the floor. I looked down where the shards should be, but they weren't there. The table was sitting upright again. Lying next to my phone on the table was the necklace, the chain piled atop itself. I could see where the chain had snapped and left the clasp still attached but broken from where it should have been linked. Jake must have picked up the table and put my phone and the necklace on it.

I didn't want to touch it. My skin crawled thinking of it lying next to me all night, but I didn't want to touch it to get rid of it. If I threw it away, would Delilah leave me alone? The necklace had brought her. It stood to reason if I destroyed it that she'd vanish, but how would I destroy it? Melt it down? Throwing it away didn't seem final enough. I glanced toward the bathroom. I could flush it and hope that did the trick. But what if it didn't? Then I would have no way of getting the necklace back to do it right.

Maybe I wouldn't have to do anything. Maybe Jake breaking the necklace took care of it all. I reached inside my mind, closed my eyes, and searched for Delilah. I didn't feel her there. Could it really be over?

I swept my hand across the table, and the necklace flew about half the distance to the wall where it had been when Jake picked it up. I'd deal with it tomorrow, but tonight, I'd sleep free of it.

With a smile and a sigh of what felt a lot like joy, I walked to the bathroom and filled the glass I kept on the sink counter. The first swallow hurt so badly that I clutched at my neck, but the second and third weren't as bad. I'd just refilled the glass when I glanced at my reflection in the mirror above the sink. I hadn't bothered with the overhead light since the nightlight was illuminating the small space. The ugly red line around my throat looked angry and slightly raised. The skin was scraped where I'd dug my nails in. It'd take days to go away.

As I turned to go back to bed, a blue light drew my attention to the mirror. The light began as a pinpoint, almost like it was actually a hole poked in the back of the glass. But it didn't stay small for long. It grew larger, a solid circle of azure, before it spread into an oval and split in two, becoming two smaller ovals that began to resemble—No! No! No!

Bright blue eyes shined from the mirror, holding me transfixed. Delilah's voice, came into my head.

"Hurt them, Ria, or I will keep hurting you. The only way to free yourself is to free me."

Chapter 39

"You sure you want to do this? You don't have to come with me. I'll be fine." I was staring up at Jonathan Ezra's house. A fine mist made everything more ominous than it already felt. The gray sky threatened with a low rumble, and I pulled up the hood of my sweatshirt. I didn't turn to look at Rachel, who had driven me in her grandma's car, and I probably shouldn't have bothered asking the question because it had actually been Rachel's idea to come over here.

I slept on the couch in the family room for the rest of the night after seeing Delilah's ethereal eyes in my bathroom mirror and called Rachel as soon as thought she was sure to be up. Since it was Saturday, I'd probably woken her anyway, though. After I told her what had happened with Jake and the necklace and then the bathroom, she'd come right over. Mom hadn't even been up yet when Rachel knocked quietly at the front door.

"Yes, I do. I want to get to the bottom of this as much as you." When I gave her a side glance, she rolled her eyes and smiled. "Okay, maybe not quite as much as you, but I do wanna know."

I thought about the necklace still lying in my bedroom floor. "I don't want you to get hurt." I dropped my gaze and tugged at the front of the oversized sweatshirt I'd put on over my leggings this morning. After what happened last night, I was scared Delilah would find a way to hurt Rachel for helping. If someone had told me a few months ago that I'd be standing in front of a house I was about to break into afraid of the ghost that had attached itself to me, I'd have hit him with my ACT study book. But here I was. Still, as badly as I needed answers, breaking into a house seemed like a pretty serious offense, and it made me nervous to think about getting caught. But it didn't seem to be bothering Rachel all that much.

Instead of replying, Rachel started up the walkway toward the massive house where my fate had become inexplicably entwined with Delilah's. We had no idea if anything would even be left in the house or if anyone would be living there, but we decided we needed to go in hopes that something or someone could help us. If nothing else, I wanted to look around. So we decided to get inside, one way or another. Even if we had to break in, we were getting in there.

Rachel tried the front door, but the knob wouldn't turn. She shrugged. "It was worth a shot."

"Maybe we should be sneaking around more." I glanced over my shoulder to see if anyone was around. Set far off the road at the end of a long drive, the house was somewhat secluded. We'd driven all the way to the door and parked on the side beneath a couple of big oak trees. Esther's car would have been hard to spot from the main road, but I still didn't want to have the police show up. Calling my parents from the police station definitely didn't sound like a great way to spend a Saturday.

Rachel stepped to the sidelight window on the left of the door and cupped her hands around her eyes in an attempt to see inside. "I can't see much, but it looks like there are still boxes in the foyer." She dropped her hands and walked past me off the porch. "Let's check around back."

I shook my head for a minute at her retreating purple hoodie. Her ponytail bounced merrily as though she weren't about to commit a felony—well, a misdemeanor anyway. "Wait for me." I jogged down the steps and caught up with her as she turned the corner. "You sure this is your first crime? You seem awfully

...confident." I shouldered into her, and she turned to me with a grin.

"I'll never tell." She stopped to try a window that was chest level. "Hope there isn't like a silent alarm going off somewhere."

I gasped. "You think there might be?" I grabbed her elbow and pulled her back from the window.

She shrugged again. "I doubt it. Nobody's lived here in awhile, and Thomasville isn't exactly a hotbed of illegal activity. Come on." Basically ignoring my concern, she trotted on, checking another couple of windows until we reached the back of the house and a less-impressive door with a grid of windows, the kind you might find in a kitchen or leading into a garage.

Rachel tried the knob, and like the front, it was locked. Looking down, she lifted the corner of a welcome mat but dropped it quickly, then made a shooing motion for me to get off of the mat. She lifted the other side and dropped it, too. "No key there." Then she stood on her tiptoes to reach a small lip at the top of the door.

"Wait a second." She slid her hand along the lip, and metal clinked upon the bricks of the landing. She scooped up the key with a broad smile.

"Viola!" She held it up triumphantly. "Just like my grandma. Must be an old people thing." She handed me the key and lifted her brows. "You wanna do it?"

I took the key and turned to the knob, half expecting it not to work when I turned the key then the knob, but the door opened creakily, and we stepped into a kitchen. I pushed back my hood.

"Kind of smaller than I would have thought," Rachel said, stepping up to a tiny sink. "I would've thought a big house like this would have a huge kitchen."

I shook my head. "I don't think this is the main kitchen." I looked at the four-burner stove. "Some of these big houses have servants' quarters. I'll bet this was the servants' kitchen." Mom had told me that. I thought of all the times we'd driven past this house and all the times she said she wished she could see inside. A pang of guilt shot through me, but I shook it off and motioned Rachel on. "Let's keep moving."

We walked down a long hallway past several rooms until we emerged beside the master staircase. I'd seen it the morning of the estate sale but hadn't gone upstairs. We glanced into the rooms off the foyer and saw crates and boxes and a few pieces of furniture wrapped in clear cellophane for moving I assumed.

"These boxes are all sealed. I wish we'd thought to bring a box cutter." Rachel knelt beside one of the boxes, pulling at the tape.

I moved back to stand at the foot of the stairs. If Delilah had lived here, did that mean she'd died here?

"Rach, didn't Ms. Claudia say Delilah lived here with her grandparents?" I didn't look away from the staircase. I had a feeling I needed to go up there.

Rachel appeared at my side. "Yeah, she said she was the only young person left in that house, or something like that." Her eyes grew large as her hand came up to her mouth. "Oh my gosh! That means—"

I nodded. "She died in the attic if I can trust the vision from last night. I have to go up there."

Rachel's mouth turned down at both corners in a grimace. "Guess so."

I started to tell her she didn't have to follow even though the thought of going up there alone made me want to pee my pants, but she took my arm and started up the steps. The wood creaked with age as we climbed two full flights.

On the third-floor landing, Rachel surveyed the closed doors and turned to me. "Now where?"

"One of these has to lead to the attic." I walked to the

farthest door and tried the knob. It opened to an empty room. Rachel tried the next, and we took turns opening doors until we reached the door at the end of the hall. "This has to be it." I turned the knob and a smaller staircase stood behind it. When I flicked the switch on the wall next to me, the light barely penetrated the darkness at the bottom of the stairs.

I turned to Rachel. "Looks like we've found it." I was giving her one more chance to back out while hoping like heck she didn't.

But steadfast Rachel, whom I was beginning to love even more with every second she stuck by me, only nodded and motioned me forward. "After you."

I put a foot on the bottom step but stopped when Rachel said, "Wait."

Pulling her phone from her hoodie pocket, she pressed on the flashlight app, bringing much-needed light to the narrow stairs. Although we could probably make it up fine with no extra light because of how enclosed the space was, I wasn't about to turn down the help. Attics creeped me out on a normal day, probably from seeing too many horror movies, but when you pair an attic with a suicide AND a spirit girl who seemed more and more bent on killing you, well, let's just say I was wishing for more than a flashlight app right then.

Rachel had a death grip on the back of my sweatshirt as I started up. We were walking so closely that had the stairs been a bit wider, I'm certain we would have been on the same step. Thankfully, the staircase wasn't too long, only about ten steps, and around halfway, I could see over the short railing around the top of the opening.

The space wasn't as large as I'd have thought considering the size of the house, but I supposed it didn't stretch across the entire top. It was stacked with boxes and trunks, some open and some sealed. A single bulb hung from the center of the room, exactly like my vision.

"I think this is it," I said. I pointed to a beam to the right of the bulb. "There." My mind's eye could easily see the horror I'd witnessed as Delilah kicked the chair from beneath her. I rubbed my neck that still hurt from my near strangling.

Rachel squeezed closer to me, her hand gripping my sleeve now. "Can you tell by looking, or are you having some kind of vibe?"

"Both." I moved to stand under the beam and looked up. Delilah's face, ashen and blue-tinged, flashed quickly above me, dead eyes staring down. I jumped, but Rachel didn't notice. She'd moved across the room to open an antique steamer trunk. As she began lifting out clothes and hats, I crossed to the other side and wiped my clammy hands on my thighs. I wasn't sure how long I wanted to stay in this room, but I couldn't leave now, not until we looked around.

"Do you know what we're looking for?" Rachel asked, filing through a stack of yellowed envelopes.

"Not really." I knelt before a cardboard box. "Anything to do with Delilah, I guess."

For the next hour, we sifted through the boxes and tried to avoid the creepy crawlies that had taken up residence in every conceivable space. I'd almost given up hope when Rachel called out.

"Come look at this!" Her voice came from behind a bureau sitting near a corner.

I pushed aside the wooden milk crate I'd been searching and went toward her. When I rounded the bureau, she was pulling out a cardboard box. "P. Ezra!" She pointed to the writing on top of the box. The dusty box was sealed with clear tape, and written beneath the name was 7753021 and 1988. "It's not her, but it may have something good in it. Ms. Claudia said Philip died a year or two after he graduated. If 1988 is a year, that would fit."

I dropped to my knees and pulled at the tape where it had curled up slightly at one edge. The dried out adhesive came off with little effort, and Rachel squatted next to the other side of the box.

Judging by the jumbled contents, the box had been tossed around. I could see photographs, a notebook, a couple of pens, a rumpled blue and pink striped shirt, a pair of jeans, some brown worn loafers, a tan folder, and some envelopes that I guessed contained letters since they were all postmarked and stamped.

I lifted a letter and studied the address. The recipient was Philip, and beneath his name was "Dura House" with a street name in Salem, Massachusetts. "Dura House? Does that sound like a college?" I asked, and before I could say anything else, Rachel was typing it into her phone.

"It's an institution, like a mental institution." She turned the phone toward me, and I saw a red brick building with white columns and a manicured lawn.

I flipped through all the envelopes. Each had the same recipient address with no return address but the same handwriting, and even though I felt a little slimy doing it, I opened one of the envelopes. The paper was a cream-colored unlined page, thicker than notebook paper, stationary paper. The letters talked about mundane, everyday things: a dinner date with another family, a recent illness, a page and a half of 'normal.' It was signed "Love always, Dad."

"These are from Philip's dad. Here." I handed her the envelopes. "Let's put these in date order." She nodded and took the envelopes while I dove back into the box, pulling out the clothes and laying them to the side so I could better see the rest of the box. The photos had tiny holes in the top corners. Pin holes. If Philip had been in an institute, he probably wasn't allowed to have frames. I imagined them hanging on a corkboard.

One of the photos showed Philip and a pretty blonde girl, the wind blowing strings of hair across her face. The two were sitting on a rock, a blue sky behind them, selfie-style as though he'd held the camera himself at arm's length. I put the photo on top of the clothes and reached for another.

The second showed Philip with his arms around the shoulders of two guys, one on either side of him. They all had on university t-shirts and were standing in front of a tent set up in a sea of others. A grill was to the left of one guy, and he was holding a spatula while burgers and hot dogs smoked on the top. The other guy held a football. People in the background were holding brown bottles or red cups, and one guy had his face painted gold and maroon. It looked like a tailgate party, and Philip's smile was as bright as the sun shining down on the scene.

The last photo was Philip in a black cap and gown, holding a blue leather-looking diploma case. An older man in a dark suit and an older woman in a floral skirt and white blouse stood to his right, smiling proudly while an unsmiling brunette stood to his left. It was Delilah. I recognized the background as the front of our high school.

I lined the photos up. High school graduation, college, girlfriend. I wasn't positive I had it correct, but it made sense. He looked so happy. How had a regular, well-rounded guy ended up in a mental hospital?

"Done," Rachel said. She handed me the stack of letters she'd arranged.

I scanned the pages as she looked in the box. They seemed like regular news from home, as though Philip's father were trying to throw Philip a normalcy lifeline. Four months of weekly letters.

"Check this out." Rachel handed across the tan folder. Philip's name and the same number on the top of the box were typed on a white sticker at the folder's edge. Attached to the inside of the cover was a photo of Philip, a very different

Philip than the one smiling in the photos. He was thin, and dark circles rimmed his once brilliant blue eyes. His cheeks were gaunt, and he looked as though he'd aged ten years. The top sheet was a check-in page with 'Dura House Intake Form' across the top. The pages beneath were doctors' notes and session updates. Prescriptions and effects were on a separate page, and at the very back was a death certificate with cause of death listed as hanging.

Rachel moved to sit beside me so that we could peruse the pages together. I felt her eyes on my face and looked up.

"This box is from the hospital," she said. "These are his personal items from his time there."

I nodded. "Yeah, I think you're right. He hanged himself."

"Just like her. Can't be a coincidence. But why?" She held up the graduation photo and the photo of Philip at the tailgate party. "How did he go from this to …that?" She motioned to the box, encompassing all the grief that would drive a handsome guy with lots of friends to hang himself. "What could have made him lose it?"

I took the graduation photo from Rachel's hand, and I knew. It wasn't what had driven him crazy. It was who.

"What would make a guy who seemed to have everything, to be totally in control, go crazy? What would make him lose his mind so that his dad kept trying to reconnect him to reality? What would make him push away the people who loved him?" I turned the photo toward Rachel and pointed at Delilah. "She would. She did it to him."

"How? She died more than a year before him, right?"

"The same way she's doing it to me. She haunted him into it."

And then the light went out.

CHAPTER 40

We moved faster than either of us knew possible to get out of that house. We didn't even bother to put Philip's belongings back into the box. As soon as the light went out in the attic, we jumped up and ran. I still had the photo of Philip and his family in my hand when I reached the back porch where we'd entered. The servants' kitchen door was still open when we got down there.

I stood with my hands on my knees, gulping air into my burning lungs. Rachel leaned against the brick wall beside the door, her breathing just as harsh as mine.

"What happened?" she heaved out between drags of air.

"I don't know. Maybe the bulb just finally burned out?" I stood and leaned next to her.

Her forehead wrinkled as she turned to me. "The bulb?"

"Yeah, that's probably why it went off." My heart still hammered, but I was beginning to catch my breath. My fingers tingled a little, like oxygen was finally making its way back into my extremities.

She shook her head. "The light didn't go out. I ran when you ran. Is that what you think happened?"

"It went out, Rach."

"No, it didn't." She tugged my hand, and we walked out into the big back lawn.

"What are we doing?" I asked, but Rachel kept walking until we had a view of the upper windows. Sure enough, light came through the tiny window at the top of the house, highlighted by the darkening sky.

She pointed up. "See."

I rubbed my temples. I was certain the light had gone out. I'd hoped without the necklace that Delilah's hold on my brain would be gone. I'd seen her that night in my bathroom mirror, but I'd hoped leaving the necklace in my room would keep her away. Apparently, she'd made me think the light had gone out, or maybe I was truly losing it.

"When you took off, I freaked and ran with you, but the light didn't go out. I can't believe I'm about to say this, but we have to go in and turn it out." She touched the edge of the photo I was gripping. "And put that back."

I sighed heavily and shook my head. "I can't go back in there."

Rachel put her hands on her hips. "Well, I don't wanna go alone! Should we just lock up and leave it? Put the picture on the kitchen counter? That sounds like a much better plan."

"They'll know someone was in there if we do that."

Rachel's brows slid up to her hairline. "Do you care?"

I looked back at the photo, at Delilah's sullen face then at Philip so full of promise on that day. He didn't deserve what happened to him. He didn't deserve to be driven crazy by a vengeful spirit. Just like me. "Yeah, I do."

I marched across the lawn, dragging a reluctant Rachel behind me.

****

To say Rachel wasn't happy about going back into the Ezra house was an understatement. She'd gone with me but had huffed in muttered tones all the way back home. I was afraid we'd be back to not speaking, and I wasn't sure I'd blame her. We'd taken the photo back to the attic, put everything back in the box, and turned out the light, locking the kitchen door on our way out. But later that night, she came to see Jake, and everything was normal—as normal as it had been anyway since Delilah had come into my life.

I put the necklace into my jewelry box. Rachel told me to get rid of it, but something told me not yet. I just hoped that something wasn't Delilah tricking me. I spent hours online that night, looking at all those sites that had scared me the first time I'd searched. I was certain Delilah had done this same thing to Philip, haunted him literally to death, and I wasn't going to go as easily as he had. I would find a way to get rid of her.

The problem with my internet searches was how much to believe. Some of the sites were completely cheesy, and the credible ones wanted to come investigate the home. I knew Mom would not agree to that, and I really didn't want to ask. I'd gotten myself into this mess despite Rachel's assurances that I hadn't chosen to be haunted, and I didn't want Mom to know. I always handled my problems. I was the smart kid, the one who could take care of herself and anyone else who came along. But as I scanned the sixth or seventh site, I was beginning to doubt that. I was a minor; an adult would have to give permission for any of these people to help me.

I pulled out my Bible, used the concordance in the back, and read the verses about casting out demons. But I didn't have the divine power bestowed to the Disciples nor their faith. I should've listened more all those years during Sunday school and preaching. I might never have been attacked if I'd been a better Christian. At this point, I was afraid I might not even have God on my side because I felt responsible for letting this thing into my life. But all of that self-abuse was useless now.

I thought again of Esther, Rachel's grandmother. She'd spent years watching shows about the supernatural. She may not be an expert, but she undoubtedly knew more than I did. I made up my mind to go see her soon. She might be my last hope.

CHAPTER 41

Rachel set her lunch tray onto the gray cafeteria table and slid her bum next to me on the red bench seat while I unwrapped my ham and cheese sandwich. I offered her half, but she shook her head and picked up her slice of cheese pizza, dipping it in the ranch dressing that dripped over the side of her tray.

I wrinkled my nose. "That's pretty nasty. How do you eat that junk?"

She covered her mouth while she talked and chewed at the same time. "I love pizza day! It's my favorite. Wanna bite?" She shoved the triangle in my face, but I drew back.

"I've got enough problems right now without adding heartburn to them." I glanced across the crowded room. "Where's Jake?" Normally Jake beat us to the cafeteria because he had study hall fourth hour, and they always left earlier than any other class.

Rachel shrugged. "Not sure," she said around another mouthful. "He didn't say he'd be late."

About that time, Jake entered from the far door followed by Coach Joseph. I hadn't had anymore episodes in his class, and the more I thought of what Delilah had shown me, the more I doubted it was possible that he'd ever been the gigantic bully she'd made him out to be. It was way more likely that she'd been jealous of his closeness with Philip and his popularity. Maybe she'd felt betrayed when Philip went away, and she was left out of the loop completely. As punishment, she'd driven Philip crazy the same way she was trying to do to me.

Jake was nodding at something Coach was saying, and without warning, everything shifted in my mind. Coach looked like he had in my previous visions, young with dark hair. Jake became the red-haired Paul Shiloh, and the two were laughing loudly in a strange, slow-motion way. The room around them blurred, like a bad photo, and all I could hear was their laughter, then they were looking at me, their laughter dying and becoming hateful sneers.

Delilah's voice rang through my head. "Hurt them, Ria. Hurt them for me."

I shook my head. She had shown me what she wanted me to see. None of it had been real except her own self-induced misery. She almost used me to do something horrible that would have ruined my life in a misguided revenge plot. I wouldn't believe her anymore. I wouldn't accept what she was showing me. My chest tightened. "No, I won't."

The voice was louder, and bright blue eyes superimposed themselves over the two boys. "Hurt them, and I will free you."

Sweat beaded on my forehead, and my chest was so tight I struggled to draw a breath. I couldn't speak, could hardly breathe.

"Then I'll take you," she said, and pain went through my head so intensely that my vision and the vision she was showing me went dark. I grabbed my head as though the pain might be stopped with the pressure of my hands.

Dimly, I was aware of someone pulling at my hands, but the pain consumed me. It throbbed like a drum in my head. A voice permeated the fog of pain.

"What's wrong? What's happening?"

I squeezed my eyes tighter, but the pain remained. I had to get her out of my head.

Rachel whisper-yelled close to my ear. "I'm here! Listen to my voice!"

I grabbed for her and latched onto her forearm. The pain intensified.

"Fight her! Don't give in to her!" Rachel's voice became louder in my head, and the pain throbbed less. "Open your eyes."

I fought the wave that threatened to pull me under and did as Rachel said. I looked into her golden eyes as she squeezed my hand. She nodded. "Good. Push her out of your head."

I imagined that I was pushing an enormous boulder up a hill, and with each inch, the pain lessened. "Keep pushing." And when the boulder reached the top of the hill, I gave one last shove and sent it and the pain sailing down.

When my vision cleared, Rachel's face came into focus, and the normal noise of the cafeteria flooded back. Tension shown in lines around her eyes and the tight line of her lips. "It's time to talk to my gram."

I nodded, and with the movement, nausea assaulted me. I took a couple of deep breaths to calm my heart and get rid of the sickness. "I couldn't agree more."

PART III

ROMANS 12:21
BE NOT OVERCOME OF EVIL, BUT
OVERCOME EVIL WITH GOOD.

CHAPTER 42

"What makes you girls think I'll be able to help?" Esther poured decaf coffee into a mug, added sugar and creamer, and sat down at her kitchen table opposite from me. Her bangles clinked happily against her enamel watch band as she raised the cup to her berry-tinted lips. She was in full makeup at 6:00 pm on a random Tuesday night. Her salt-and-pepper hair was stiff with products, and she looked as though she was going out on a date in her plum pants and floral silk blouse. Windowed ten years ago, a date wasn't an impossibility for Esther. Rachel said she's the toast of the country club's Senior Scooters, a dance group for the local fifty-plus crowd.

We'd just spent an hour telling her everything that had happened since the estate sale, from Ruth Claudia who didn't even remember buying the necklace to my most recent brush with Delilah in the cafeteria yesterday. Aside from her wide eyes when I told her about smashing the mirror and my near choking, she'd been quiet and let me talk.

"Gram, you're our only option." Rachel leaned against the counter, her booted feet crossed and as she ran her finger up and down the long gold-tone chain she wore. With her purple sweater and pink lip gloss, it was clear they were related. Rachel's glossy black hair would undoubtedly look like Esther's someday. They shared the same honey eyes, and if Rachel was lucky, her face would look as smooth as her gram's at that age.

Esther swung those golden eyes at Rachel. "No, you could tell her mother. *That* is another option." Rachel stood up straight and looked to me for support.

I pulled nervously at my fingers, leaning forward against the table. I had to convince Esther to help me even if she wasn't an expert. She was as close as I had since it was impossible from an online search to tell the real deal from the phonies. "Ms. Esther, I just want your opinion. That's all, your opinion. If you were watching this on one of your shows, what would they do? How would they help the stupid girl who got herself into this?" I dropped my gaze to the wooden tabletop until I felt the brush of Esther's soft hand against mine.

"I know you've been through quite an ordeal, sweetie." Her gentle smile nearly brought tears to my eyes. "But those are only television shows." She chuckled. "And mostly not very good ones. They probably aren't even real people."

Rachel pulled out the chair beside mine and sat down. "You just said the magic word, Gram—probably. They may be fake, but what if they aren't? What if some of them are true?"

Esther shook her head, but I could almost see a shift in her. She quirked up one side of her mouth as her eyes went to Rachel, then back to me. She took a drink of coffee, then leaned back in her chair and crossed her arms. "Well, if this becomes an episode of *Ghost Warriors*, you two better make sure someone good plays my part, someone forty with fabulous taste."

I smiled at Rachel, knowing we'd at least get a little advice if not a solution. Relief warred with common sense as I tried not to be hopeful. I was about to take the advice of a woman whose claim to expertise came from her DVR. No, Esther wasn't even claiming that. We forced her to be our authority on paranormal occurrences. The sad thing was, this wasn't the craziest thing that had happened in the last month. I almost laughed. Almost.

"What you really need is a priest. They always call in a priest when things get this bad." She leaned forward, her arms on the table and her hands cupping her coffee mug.

Rachel and I exchanged a look. A priest? I didn't know a priest. I knew there was a Catholic church in town, and some of the kids at school were Catholic, but I wasn't sure how I'd go about getting in touch with a priest. Assuming he'd agree to meet with me, I'd have to go through this whole story with him and then pray (no pun intended) that he'd help me.

"Do you know one?" Rachel asked.

"Not really. I mean, I know of one, but I don't really know him. I've only been to the Catholic church once, and that was two years ago for Candace's wedding, remember that?" She smiled at Rachel. "Remember how beautiful she looked? And all those roses! Oh my, bet it cost your great-uncle Aaron a fortune!"

Rachel shook her head. "Focus, Gram. Catholic church?"

She waved her right hand and lifted her mug with her left. "Yes, yes, sorry, dear. That was my one and only time. So I'm not going to be helpful on that end, girls." She took a sip, and my hopes went down faster than her coffee. But her face lit up suddenly. She set down her cup. "But I really think you two might have stumbled on your solution without my help."

"We did?" I looked at Rachel, whose face looked as confused as I felt.

Esther nodded. "You said that when this—" she waved her hand around again as though that would help her define what to call Delilah "—thing was in your head yesterday in the cafeteria you managed to chase her out."

"Well, yes, I suppose I did." I wasn't following what Esther was getting at.

Her index finger moved between Rachel and me. "The two of you."

"The two of us?" Rachel sat back in her chair and pointed to herself. "I didn't do anything."

"Think back to what you told me. You said the two of you

were sitting together when Ria's vision shifted, and you talked to her and helped her push away the vision."

"Yeah, so? All I did was tell her to fight back."

Esther looked at me. "That might be your answer. When you broke into the Ezra house, Rachel was able to show you that the light was still on." She slanted her eyes in Rachel's direction. "Breaking and entering is something I intend to revisit with you, young lady, when all this is over." Looking back at me, she continued, "If she hadn't been there, what would you have done?"

I lifted one shoulder in a shrug. "I suppose I would have run out and never looked back."

"And when the chain was choking you, what happened to break the connection?"

"Jake, we told you that, Gram." Rachel's brows couldn't get any closer together, or they'd be touching.

"Right." She nodded and sipped her coffee again, as if that answered all our questions.

After exchanging another look, Rachel motioned her hand in a get-on-with-it movement. "Drawing a blank here."

Esther rolled her eyes as though we were five-year-olds who couldn't figure out how to shut the door. "Family and friends. That was this girl's problem, wasn't it? She was jealous or lonely or whatever. She didn't think she had friends, and she was envious of her brother. You have both. Use them."

"Use them how?" I asked.

She nodded once. "Force her away with the bonds you have with Jake and Rachel."

Rachel tilted her head. "But how, Gram?"

She pursed her lips and looked up, then back at us. "I have no idea."

CHAPTER 43

Rachel stood at the top of the attic stairs in the Ezra house. "Yep, just like we left it. Tell me again why you think we have to be *here* to do this."

"Whoa, this is creepy without the whole 'hang yourself from the rafters' story." Jake turned a circle, taking in the entire room.

When I told Rachel I thought we should go back to the scene of Delilah's death, I feared she'd bolt. I would if I'd been her but not solid, steady Rachel. Complain? Yes, but she'd been there for me since I finally told her the truth about what was happening, and it looked as though she'd be here till the end of this madness—what I hoped would be the end, anyhow.

I balked at Esther's suggestion at first. How could we banish an apparition with friendship and family? That was the last thing I'd expected. It sounded like something you'd find on a funny meme, not an actual idea, but Rachel had been there even though all of this was completely crazy. Maybe Gram was onto something after all.

I wasn't so sure about Jake's role. He'd listened, one brow raised incredulously the entire time, then laughed until he realized neither of us were joking, and we weren't going to leave him alone till he agreed to at least try.

Jake peeked into a couple of the boxes against the far wall. "Don't we need a stake or silver bullets or something?"

Rachel rolled her eyes. "That's vampires and werewolves."

"And we have all the silver we need." I held up the necklace and let it dangle from my fist. I still wasn't sure what to do, but the necklace had been the beginning, and I felt like it would bring the end.

"So, what do we do now?" He threw up both hands before letting them drop back to his sides, like the only bigger waste of his time would be shoe shopping with Mom. "I'm still not sure I believe all this, but I'm here. So what do I do?"

Rachel put her hands on her hips. "How can you not believe it? You saw her the other night. You saved her for goodness sake!"

"Yeah, I saw her, and yeah, she's been weird, but when I told her I wanted to know what was going on, I thought she'd tell me she was on drugs or something, not being haunted." He threw up his hands again.

"You'd prefer the drugs?" I shook my head. If we weren't standing in a house we'd broken into twice, in a room where a girl committed suicide, waiting for a dangerous ghost to show up, I'd have laughed. Then again, that might have been easier.

"Well, yeah! You can touch drugs. You lay 'em down, and they're there when you go look for them. You can go to rehab for drugs. We can tell Mom and Dad, get real help." He held out both hands and spun in a slow circle. "This? This is nuts!"

We stared at each other for a minute till he dropped his gaze. I walked toward him. "I know it's crazy. Believe me, I get it. I've been trying to convince myself it isn't real for a month. I have to try, and I think I need you, Bub." I rested my hand on his forearm.

His shoulders slumped in defeat, and he sighed heavily. "I'm here, ain't I." He quirked one side of his mouth in a half-smile. "But I don't have to like it or believe it. No way Coach would ever do any of what you told me you saw in those visions, but if this is what you think you need, I'll do it, whatever it is we're actually doing."

It had been years since Jake had told me he loved me, but in that minute, I knew that's what he was saying. By being here, he was doing the best he could to tell me he loved me. "I know you will. I just wish I knew exactly what to do."

Rachel's forehead wrinkled in thought as she looked toward the area where we found Philip's box of belongings. "When we were here before, you thought the light had gone out when we were going through Philip's stuff. Should we get it all back out again? That might trigger something." She looked to me for confirmation.

I nodded. "Good idea."

"Wait. We're gonna 'trigger' activity? Is that a good idea?" Jake asked, looking more uncomfortable by the minute.

"Thought you didn't believe." Rachel tilted her head and gave him a sideways glance.

He crammed his hands into the pocket of his navy hoodie but missed the nonchalance vibe by a mile. "I don't—mostly."

Laying the necklace over the edge, I lifted the box and brought it to the center of the room beneath the hanging bulb and sat in front of it. Pulling out the belongings sent a chill down my spine. With each item, my shoulders tightened with tension, torn between not wanting anything to happen and needing something to happen. I had to get Delilah to show herself if I had any hope of this working, but the thought of seeing her had my stomach in knots.

Rachel motioned for Jake to sit, and the two flanked me on either side. When we were here before, we hadn't made it to the bottom of the box, but this time, I took out everything. Besides the medical records, clothes, and photos, there were a few charcoal sketches—flowers, trees, landscape stuff—and a yearbook.

"It's Philip's yearbook." Rachel picked up the book with its familiar neon 'T' on the front. "Wonder why this is in the box?"

I shook my head and stared down at the photo of Philip and his family. "He probably asked his parents to bring it when they visited."

"Yeah but why?" She motioned to the small mound in front of us. "He had so few personal items." She held up the yearbook.

"He won everything, was an officer in a ton of clubs. I'll bet his room was covered in plaques and trophies. You know he had other mementos his parents could have brought. Why would he ask for this?"

She was right. His parents could have given him a dozen other things. He must have had a reason for wanting it. I spread the three photos from the box in front of me. The photos of Philip at the tailgate party and him with Angel's mother represented his present at the time he was institutionalized. The graduation photo was a part of his past but *only* a part. To a twenty-year-old, high school friends would seem almost as important as family.

I took the book from Rachel's hands. "I'm sure Delilah was showing Philip visions, too. If you were stuck in an institute and you needed to connect with the people in your visions, what would you do?"

"I'd ask them to visit," Rachel said.

I shrugged. "Who's to say he didn't? Maybe they couldn't visit."

"Or wouldn't," Jake said, picking up the file and opening it. "Maybe his parents found a way to stop any other visitors. They were kind of important, right? They'd be embarrassed to have a son in the nuthouse."

Rachel narrowed her eyes at him, pursing her lips like Esther. "Jake! Not nice."

He lifted one shoulder, then flipped through the papers in the file.

"Jake could be right. They probably didn't want other people to see their golden boy like that." I pointed to the file. "Regardless of the why, if Philip needed to connect to those people or those days and couldn't see them physically, this book may have been his connection."

Rachel picked up a pencil sketch of the front of Dura House.

Her eyes scanned the page, her fingers drifting to the bottom right corner where Philip had signed his name. "It's so sad. He was trapped in an institution with no one except a family who was likely keeping anyone else from contacting him."

"You have to remember they already had a child who committed suicide. I'm sure Delilah's death was beyond shocking." I picked up the graduation photo and looked closely at Delilah. Her unsmiling face made me sad and angry at the same time. Her feelings had left behind this vengeful spirit who was hellbent on hurting people who probably hadn't done anything to her. Every teenager alive could sympathize with feeling like an outcast, but most don't resort to wanting to kill those who made them feel that way. And in the process, she'd driven her brother to do the exact same thing she'd done.

Rachel laid the drawing down on the wooden floor. "Yeah, but to leave your son stuck in some home?"

Jake tossed down the folder. "Pretty crappy family."

As soon as he said it, the single light flickered. Rachel's wide-eyed face turned to me, and I knew she'd seen it, too. This time it wasn't just me.

"Was that—did she do that?" Jake's head was on a swivel, turning to take in all the dark corners of the attic.

I wasn't positive until I felt my hands and face go cold as my stomach churned. I had to bring her out in the open, out of my head. "What's wrong, Delilah? Don't like Jake talking about your family?" I spoke loudly and stood. "You hated them, right? You killed yourself and your brother because you felt so alone, didn't you?" The light flickered again, then grew brighter till the bulb made a popping sound and went out completely.

Rachel crawled behind me to squeeze close to Jake.

Grabbing the necklace, I stepped over the box and stood directly beneath the rafter where Delilah hanged herself. "We can't talk about them? About Philip?" For about thirty seconds, nothing happened, and I was beginning to think she wouldn't show, but a rattling in the corner had us all spinning in that direction. I stepped toward the sound.

"Don't go over there!" Rachel whisper-yelled as I walked to a stack of three boxes.

I didn't turn around. I looked up as though I'd see Delilah perched on the rafters. "I'm here. What do you want from me now? I'm tired of being your puppet." The rattling increased, and I moved the top two boxes. Behind the boxes leaning against the wall was an oval shape covered by a dusty drop cloth. I had a feeling I knew what it was, but I shoved the necklace in my front pocket and used both hands to lift it free and bring it back to where I'd seen it in my vision. I jerked the drop cloth aside, and there was the mirror where Delilah had put the necklace before climbing onto that chair. The mirror was my key to drawing her out. I'd seen her in the kitchen mirror then in my bedroom mirror. She would use the mirror to show her true self.

"Come on, Dee! Show yourself!" I used her brother's nickname hoping to pull her out of hiding. I was afraid, but my fear was quickly being overtaken by anger. I wasn't sure if it was my anger or hers, but it built inside like an inferno. My face grew hot, and my hands shook.

"Is that a good idea, pissing her off?" Jake's voice was strained in a way I hadn't heard since we were kids hiding from a thunderstorm in his closet.

The mirror began to rattle again, almost bouncing against the wall where it leaned. "I have to. I'm sick of being afraid. Come out, Dee!" The mirror rattled harder until it cracked loudly. It went completely still as the crack webbed across the entire surface. A blue dot of light glowed from the center.

CHAPTER 44

"There you are." I knelt in front of the broken mirror as the light grew, then split into two ovals. "I'm actually surprised you showed since you're a coward." My bravado belied the shaking in my hands and dryness in my mouth.

"Ria!" Rachel shouted. I glanced over my shoulder to see that the two of them had stood and retreated to the top step of the stairs, ready for a fast escape. I couldn't blame them. They'd never seen this. I had, and I hoped it was for the last time.

"She is. She couldn't handle her life, couldn't stand that Philip had real friends, and when he couldn't help her get her revenge, she drove him to kill himself. Now, she's attacking someone else, but this time it won't work." When the surface filled with the swirling smoke I'd seen right before my head smashed my mirror, I wasn't so sure of myself. My boldness slipped a little remembering how she'd held me against the glass, but I couldn't stop now.

The blue lights became her eyes as the smoke transformed into the shape of a girl. Her voice invaded my head. "You're scared, Ria. I can feel it."

The form became more distinct, and Delilah's face showed on the surface, colorless except for those azure eyes. Then her mouth moved, but the sound of her voice remained in my head. "All you had to do was hurt them, then I would have freed you."

My whole body shook. "No, you wouldn't have. I would end up just like you and Philip. I wouldn't have been able to live with myself if I'd done something to any of them."

"Philip left me alone. He left, and I had no one. He shouldn't have gone away." The ethereal face floated among the gray smoke, tendrils slipping out of the cracks and twirling around my knees and lower legs.

"It wasn't his fault you were weak."

The face contorted, twisting and terrifying. "I wasn't! They wouldn't accept me without him! They hurt me! You weren't there; you didn't see!"

"No, I wasn't, but neither were you. Those visions you showed me weren't real. None of it happened." The tendrils grew thicker, their coldness seeping through my jeans. I felt them pushing against my backside and twirling up my spine.

Delilah screamed, and my hands automatically went to my ears as though the sound weren't in my head. Pain exploded with the scream.

Jake bounded across the room toward me. He wrapped his arms around me and pulled, but I could still feel the cold tendrils. They tightened, and though both of us pulled against their force, my knees inched closer to the mirror.

"He can't save you! Just like Philip couldn't save me!" Delilah's voice boomed in my ears.

"Rachel, help me!" Jake pulled as Rachel's arms wrapped around me, too. "Pull!"

But their force was only enough to slow the dragging power of the smoke. Then I thought of the necklace. This had all started with my blood. When I'd cut my lip on the necklace, I'd made all this possible. Delilah might have chosen me that day at the estate sale, but I'd sealed our connection with my blood, and I felt certain this could separate us. I'd let it come this far by letting her in, and I had to break her hold.

All those images I'd seen online from the hand-drawn sketches to the oil paintings had one thing in common—blood sacrifice, innocence lost beneath the edge of a knife, or in this case, a necklace. To get power, you had to take it from someone like Delilah had. Now, I had to take it back.

"I need my hands!" I yelled so that Jake and Rachel would loosen up enough for me to get the necklace from my pocket. Yanking it out, I held it in my palm and pressed my thumb against the prongs, pushing hard until I felt the bite of them against my skin. I lifted my thumb enough to see the blood and squeezed it with my index finger until the drops came freely, and I smeared it all over the surface of the clover.

"You can't hold me anymore! It's over, Delilah!" I slammed the pendant into the center of the mirror. "Pull!" I screamed to Jake and Rachel.

The tendrils increased until I was sure they must be wrapping around all three of us, and the blue light shone so brightly that I squeezed my eyes closed against the force of it. Delilah roared in my head, but I held the pendant to the mirror. Suddenly the pressure of the tendrils snapped, and all three of us fell backward in a heap as the blue light glowed even brighter until it exploded, and the glass exploded into dust over us all.

The quiet of the room echoed in my head. Our heavy breathing was the only sound, and we all lay unmoving for a minute.

"Is she gone? Is it over?" Rachel asked, sitting up slowly and brushing off the glass dust.

Jake sat up and pulled me up with a hand on my upper arm. I didn't trust my legs to hold just yet, so I crawled to the mirror. The glass was completely gone, and the necklace lay on the floor, my blood gone from the surface.

Rachel knelt next to me. "It's clean. Where did it go?"

I didn't have an answer. I could only shake my head.

"Did we get rid of her?" Jake stood behind me.

I searched inside of my head, and it was all quiet for the first time since I'd stepped into this house weeks ago. "I think so. I think we did it." I got to my feet and faced them before launching myself at them both, pulling them against me in a monster hug. When I felt both sets of arms reach around me this time, I let the tears come with a laugh.

Thanks to my brother and my friend, I had my sanity back.

Jake pulled back enough to look at me. "Can we go home now and pretend none of this happened?"

"Absolutely!" I stepped away and wiped my face with my palms. "But first, I've got one more thing to do."

I walked over to the Philip's box.

"What are you doing?" Rachel asked.

"Closing the loop." I placed everything back inside, dropping the necklace on top of the pile before pulling the edges of the box back together. I stood and stepped back to the center of the room. "Rest in peace, Ezra children."

Then we started down the attic steps, and something inside told me we wouldn't have to come back again.

EPILOGUE

"Just set the rest of them over there." Angel Ezra pointed to a corner of her study. Her townhouse was bursting at the seams with the leftover boxes from her great-grandfather's house. She'd only saved a few important pieces of his enormous collection for herself, but the boxes packed with what didn't sell as well as those from his attic were taking up a lot of real estate. She was determined to go through it all before her wedding next month.

"Thanks." She gave the movers a tip and closed the door behind them, turning with a sigh to survey the mountain of boxes.

Her grandparents, Samuel and Lois, had more or less dumped all of this in her lap, but in all fairness, she had put it off for far too long. She couldn't tell them no. They'd raised her, given her the best education, and bought her this townhouse. She would finish this in the next few days, keep what she wanted, and give away the rest if need be.

Pulling back her dark hair into a messy bun, she grabbed a box from the top of a stack and hauled it to the floor in front of her leather sofa. She sat behind the box and noticed for the first time that it had writing on the top. The flaps on the top of the box had been pulled together in a way that held the box closed without tape.

P. Ezra, 7753021, 1988. P. Ezra? That had to be Philip; this box held her father's belongings. She'd never known him. He'd died when her mother was pregnant, and her grandparents had convinced her mother to sign over her parenting rights to them since Philip was dead. She'd never seen either of her parents in person, and her grandparents didn't like to talk about Philip, at least not the Philip who'd killed himself. They would only talk about the Philip who'd been a high school star.

She pulled out a stack of clothes, a folder, some sketches, and three photographs. She studied the faces of her father and mother. Lois had shown her a copy of this same photo when Angel had been about ten and started to ask questions. But to see it here in a box of his belongings brought a flood of sadness. She laid the photo aside and picked up the other two. She glanced at the photo of Philip with some other guys, but she looked closely at the graduation photo. She'd seen this one before, too.

Aunt Delilah was an even deeper mystery than her father. Her grandparents were strong people to have lived through the suicides of both of their children, and she'd said so once to her grandfather, who'd told her she had been their saving grace. That's why they'd named her Angel.

She opened the file and saw the photo inside, the face aged so much from the smiling boy in the photos, and she quickly flipped it closed, not wanting to read it right now. She couldn't let this bog her down. After the wedding and honeymoon, she'd pick it back up but not now.

Something glinted at the bottom of the box. A silver chain peeked from beneath the corner of a yearbook. Moving the book, she lifted the chain from the box and held it up to her face. A silver clover hung from the chain, a fiery opal sparkling green and blue from the center. Angel put her other hand behind the pendant to get a better look at it. It was beautiful, but why was it in her father's box? Maybe it had been her mother's. Could it be a gift he'd never given her?

She walked to the mirror across the study and held the necklace against her chest above her t-shirt. It felt inexplicably warm against her skin, and she had an irrational thought that it must be her father's love. This was what she'd been looking for.

Even though she'd rolled her eyes at the old superstition, her fiancée Jonas had made her promise to do the "something old, something new, something borrowed, and something blue" thing. She had something old, borrowed, and blue taken care of, but she'd been searching for her something new.

This necklace would be her something new. It was perfect. Maybe it'd bring her good luck. She fastened the clasp and admired the way the necklace caught and held the light. She pulled out her hair tie and ran her hands through her dark hair. Her blue eyes sparkled in the mirror.

Acknowledgments

As with every novel I've written, I have to thank first and foremost my family. Chris, Olivia, and Wyatt, you give me the love and support that allows me to do what I love. Thank you for sacrificing my time to pursue this love of mine.

I also want to thank my beta readers: Katie French, Stephanie Murray, and Amy Rice. Your excitement at receiving pages kept me motivated. Elizabeth Love and Kerri Hughes, I owe you two a big thanks for taking a chance on someone you didn't even know. Kim Bounds, thank you for helping to proofread when I couldn't stand to read another line, and a BIG thanks to Samantha March for her support and proofing skills.

I want to thank God for answering—and not answering—my prayers. I'm not sure if my faith became stronger *as* I wrote the novel, or if my faith became stronger, *so* I wrote the novel. Either way, I've somehow grown in my faith over the course of this book.

Last but never least, thank you to all of my readers. This novel is not my typical genre, and I appreciate all of you who said, "Write that book" when I wasn't sure if I should or not. Thank you for taking a chance right along with me.